WORLD LITERATURE
IN TRANSLATION

ADAM SMALL

Kanna—
He Is Coming Home

Translated from Afrikaans in association with
the author with an Afterword by
CARROL LASKER

GARLAND PUBLISHING, INC.
NEW YORK & LONDON 1992

Library of Congress Cataloging-in-Publication Data

Small, Adam. 1936–
    [Kanna, hy kô hystoe. English]
    Kanna—he is coming home / Adam Small; translated in association with the
author with an afterword by Carrol Lasker.
    p. cm. — (The Garland library of world literature in translation; 17)
    Translation of: Kanna, hy kô hystoe.

    Includes bibliographical references.

    ISBN 0-8240-3312-4

    I. Title. II. Series: Garland library of world literature in translation; v. 17.
PT6592.29.M3K313   1990
839.3'62—dc20   90-3120

Printed on acid-free, 250-year-life paper
Manufactured in the United States of America

Acknowledgments

Grateful thanks to Nancy Kearns. Kwaku Amoabeng, Paul Roberge and Louise O. Vasvari for valuable assistance.

Foreword

The scenes are from our poor areas. The play is not chronological. The characters speak over distances, years, dreams, and from the dead. The title of the piece "Kanna—He Is Coming Home," must be spoken somewhat quickly to obtain the rhythmic effect of the K-H-C-H sounds.

Kanna—
He Is Coming Home

CHARACTERS

MAKIET, THE OLD WOMAN IN THE WHEELCHAIR; SHE IS HALF-BLIND. [SHE ACTS, FROM HER CHAIR WHICH SHE NEVER LEAVES, WITH HER VOICE, WITH BODY GESTURES, AND WITH HER HALF-BLIND EYES. HER SPACE DOES NOT REMAIN STATIC; OFTEN SHE MUST MOVE THE WHEELCHAIR HERSELF.]

KANNA, HER WELFARE-CHILD

KIETIE, HER DAUGHTER

DIEKIE, HER SON

PANG, HER SECOND HUSBAND, DOES NOT APPEAR

ROESYLN, WITH WHOM KANNA BOARDS WHEN HE GOES TO SCHOOL IN THE CITY

JAKOP, THE STREETPREACHER, HER SON

YSIE, HER DAUGHTER

JIENA, HER DAUGHTER

TOEFIE, HER SON, A HAWKER

SKOEN, HER SON, A HAWKER

POENA (DOES NOT APPEAR)

BOELA

BAI

SONNIE, A FRUIT PEDDLER

GUITAR PLAYERS, A FLOWER SELLER, A FEW OTHERS, VOICES

1. Oh, Where Is Moses ──────────────

Dark—then music—a single guitar, no other
instrument: "Oh, Where Is Moses"

As the light grows, JAKOP *upstage,* GUITAR PLAYERS *on*
either side of him.

He moves forward with arms outstretched.

He prays, the GUITAR PLAYERS *moving with him.*

JAKOP

Oh Where
Where
where is Moses
Moses, Moses, the stammerer
Moses, Moses, the stutterer
Moses, Moses, the murderer?
The men of the world, they panic
everywhere
But Moses simply grabbed his stick
and shouted on his people, shouted loud
and walked with them
under the fire from heaven
under that burning cloud
and Moses, Moses was a stammerer
yes Moses, Moses was a stutterer
and Moses was a murderer
But God was with him
over him and under him and on the sides
Oh Where

Where
where is Moses
Moses, Moses the stammerer
Moses, Moses the stutterer
Moses, Moses the murderer?
The men of the world take foolish chances
but Moses, simply, in a trance
walked upon the people with those two stones
and *told* them the words on those two stones
the work of God's finger and God's fire there
and said: You stand by this
You stand by this
or you fall by this
And Moses, Moses was a stammerer
and Moses, Moses was a stutterer
Oh, where
where
Where is Moses
Moses. Moses, the stammerer
Moses. Moses, the stutterer
Moses. Moses, the murderer?
The men of the world, they fake everything
but Moses lifted up the copper snake
before those difficult people
and those difficult people laughed (but they were frightened stiff)
and those difficult people lived . . . . *lived*

ECHOES

. . . . . . lived. . . . . . lived. . . . . . lived

JAKOP

And Moses was a stammerer
yes Moses was a stutterer
and Moses was a murderer
but that stutterer
that stammerer
that murderer

4

lifted up the copper snake
and those slabs of rock
and his difficult people laughed
but lived!
Oh, where
where
where is Moses
Moses, Moses, stammerer
Moses, Moses, stutterer
Moses, Moses, murderer
Where
where
where is Moses
Moses, Moses, stammerer
Moses, Moses, stutterer
Moses, Moses, the murderer?
  (*The music suddenly resounds. The stage has grown completely dark.*
    Then the music dies away under a narrator's voice.)

VOICE

Our story is about the simple ones of the earth, very ordinary people
and poor—those who will always be with us . . . .
Always
It is the story also of one who loves them.
Kanna, Makiet's adopted son, her welfare-child.
        (*The light now searches out each character,*
            stays a moment, then searches on)

First, Makiet with old Paans, her first husband, on the Karoo farm.
Then she could still work, hard with her hands, then she wasn't half
blind yet; and later, after old Paans' death, Makiet with old Pang, her
second husband, in Cape Town, District Six.....
        (*The light falls on* PANG)

She scrimped for Kanna; she had him taught so he could go to high
school in the city. She let him come and live with Auntie Roeslyn in
Cape Town.
        (*The light falls on* ROESLYN)

5

And later, old Pang had him taught even more. And Kanna learned well. Then Kanna went away, far away. From Diekie (*the light falls on* DIEKIE) and from Kietie; (*the light on* KIETIE) and from Auntie Roeslyn's children, Ysie and Jiena, and Toefie and Skoen, and Jakop; a man of God, they called Jakop, a man of God.

(*The light again falls on* JAKOP.)

The telling of our story is not chronological. The people of our story speak to each other across distances, over long years, and from the dead. Those who are close think of those far away, those who live recall those dead. . . Like Jakop. A man of God, they called him. . .

JAKOP

Oh where
where
where is Moses
Moses, Moses, stammerer
Moses, Moses, stutterer
Moses, Moses, murderer?

(*The light shines on all.*)

VOICE

And they waited for Kanna, through all the long years they waited for him. To come home.

(*The stage darkens. The sound of the softly crying southeaster.*)

2. Goodbye, Kanna ————————————————

> DIEKIE *enters, his presence first apparent from the tiny glow of his cigarette. He stands right of center, his bearing nonchalant. In the background, the suggestion of a small municipal house. Then, motionless in the dark,* DIEKIE *starts whistling jazzily, but it's a somber tune, a religious sound.*
>
> *After a while the refrain grows in volume, as guitars (no other instrument) take up the tune.* DIEKIE *has stopped whistling. The cigarette glows red. At last the music floats away in the sound of the southeaster. The wind screams thinly around the corner of the little house, a loose sheet of corrugated iron grinding on a rusty nail. Then, in bright light,* MAKIET *appears, and behind her* KANNA. *Looking timid (the impression is completely false), in the large wheelchair surrounded by the light, she is clothed in an aura of unearthliness. For a moment the two remain still; then, with the wind howling around the wheelchair, which is pushed by* KANNA, *they come downstage.*

MAKIET

The wind is strong, hey Kanna? (*pause*) Do you still remember this wind, Kanna?

> (KANNA *does not reply. They are now at stage front*)

Everything's dead and gone and over, Kanna. (*Pause*) I said everything's dead and gone and over. . .

> (*She is aware of the many people, and her words, like her half-blind eyes, seek direction.* KANNA *doesn't speak*)

Do you still remember Diekie? . . .Kanna, our Diekie. . .

> (*She has turned her eyes toward* DIEKIE)
>
> (KANNA *behind the wheelchair, and* DIEKIE'S *eyes meet*)

And Kietie? Kanna, do you still remember Kietie?

> (KIETIE *in. This time* MAKIET *does not look around her. Just like*

7

MAKIET and DIEKIE, KIETIE *is a vision. She remains standing to one side upstage. Her eyes meet* KANNA's)

KANNA

(*Finally turning away, his hands clutching the wheelchair nervously. He shakes his head in confusion, softly*)

Makiet! Makiet!
            (*She makes no answer. Remains peering with blind eyes*)

She does not answer. The dead don't answer. How can they? Only their story stays. . . .

ECHO

Only their story stays.

KANNA

I loved you.

ECHO

Their story stays.

KANNA

I loved you.

ECHO

I loved you.

KANNA

I. . . (*Pause*)

MAKIET

That's why I couldn't understand it, Kanna. . . .
But God was also merciful, after all, Kanna. . .

8

KANNA

(*Passionately*)

You must have tried to understand. . . .
(KANNA *leaves the wheelchair confusedly and moves across the stage*)

KIETIE

(*As* KANNA *approaches her, where she still stands
silently gazing across the stage, passionately*)

It was not my fault!
(*Perplexed,* KANNA *comes to a halt*)

(KIETIE *repeats, frightened*)

It wasn't my fault!

DIEKIE

(*Agitated where he also stands motionless*)

They were shit, Kanna. Real shit, the bastards! No, don't look at me
like that. I'm right, Kanna! You don't know, you wouldn't, because
you weren't here, but I was really converted, they broke it again for
me. It's true, Kanna, what I say, they were real shit, *swine*, the
bastards! You would have also said so, if you were here! It's also them
who caused old Pang's death. He was a good old man, even though he
wasn't our own father, like Paans. . . Do you still remember old Pang,
Kanna?
(PANG *in, grayish, in his lop-sided way, with the little movements
familiar to* KANNA; *as* PANG *walks, he rubs his spectacles with a
handkerchief, and so on.* PANG *laughs his little fine laughter, startling*
KANNA. *He stops, stands a little away from* KANNA *and continues
laughing with* KANNA, *that friendly, delicate little laugh.*

KANNA, *who has half hidden his face in his hands while* DIEKIE
was talking, now turns and stares at PANG. *For a long time they
stand like this, silently,* PANG *laughing.*)

9

PANG

(with a delicate voice, happily)

It was a long time, Kanna. We longed for you so much. Yes. We missed you so much. Yes. But the Lord, he was good to us, all the same, all the years. Yes.

KANNA

(Wants to say something, can't find the words. He looks from PANG to KIETIE to DIEKIE. Then aside, bitter and bewildered)

Oh my God!

MAKIET

. . . And do you still remember Paans? Shame, poor Paans. But you'll maybe not remember anymore. Little Krools, he was my oldest, but he died, only a year old, he's been lying in his little grave all these years, far away in the Karoo. There little Krools lies beside Paans, for all these years, Kanna. *(Her voice trembles)*

He would have been a man now, yes, a big grown man, if he had lived, as I say, little Krools.

(The expression on her face has become softer and it looks as if she's crying)

I was only nineteen when I had him. . . *(Dreamily)*

The years. It's been a long time, Kanna, the years. . .

KANNA

Yes, Makiet. I know.

MAKIET

The years are hard, you know, Kanna. But that's the way that God forgives people, but that's the way he answers when people pray. . . But God's mercy is hard, Kanna. He's full of mercy, all the same. *(A long pause, then suddenly impatient)*

Let them go away, Kanna!

(KANNA looks from the one to the other, where the three have remained standing. Then they exit, slowly. MAKIET shifts her chair)

KANNA
(*Staring after* KIETIE *and the others, imitates* MAKIET)

God's mercy is hard.
How do I tell them? How do I tell her? How do I? How do you tell someone that's dead now and to be buried tomorrow. . .
Makiet! (*She does not answer*) (*Again*)
Makiet! (*She does not answer*) (*Silence*) (*Cynically*)
The dead don't speak. The dead can't speak. After so many years no one cares to speak anyway. After so much has happened. . . Far too much. . . (*Pause*) Yes! They let me know about Kietie's death, and then about Diekie's. No, they didn't write, Roeslyn's daughters, because it was they who let me know. How unworldly-wise Makiet and Diekie were!

MAKIET
(*Calls*)

Ysie! Ysie! Jiena!

(*The two girls enter*)

YSIE, JIENA

Yes, Makiet?

MAKIET
(*Staring out over the audience, slowly*)

You must let Kanna know about Kietie. Maybe he can still be here for the funeral.

(YSIE *and* JIENA *look at each other*)

(*Slowly, emphatically*)

No, don't write; the letters they take too long, so don't write.

YSIE

But Makiet. . .

MAKIET

You must phone. You must phone to Kanna; then he'll come on the plane for Kietie, her funeral.

JIENA

But Makiet, it's a lot of money to phone there. . .

YSIE

It's *very* far away, Makiet.

MAKIET

(*Determined*)

Will you phone to Kanna for me, Jiena? I know it's very far away . . . (JIENA *looks at* YSIE)

JIENA

Yes, Makiet.

MAKIET

(*Fingering her dress, she produces a little purse*)

I still have my pension for two months, after all. So will you phone to Kanna for me? . . .

YSIE

Yes, Makiet.

JIENA

Yes, we'll phone to Kanna for you, Makiet.
                    (*They look at each other*)

KANNA

They did. Phone to me. For Makiet.

(Sounds of telephonic connection) *(Acts as if he is picking up the receiver of a telephone. Sounds of the telephone connection)*

Hello! Hello!

YSIE

(Pretends she is handling a telephone, nervously)

Hello, is it Kanna? Is it Kanna Davids?. . . Hey?

KANNA

Hello!

YSIE

Hello! It is Kanna Davids? It is Ysie, here, Kanna, and Jiena. Auntie Roeslyn's children! Hello, Kanna! It's about Kietie of Makiet. . . Hello! Hello!

KANNA

Hello!

YSIE

Makiet's Kietie. Kanna, she's dead, Kanna! She . . . she . . . died last night! Makiet wants to know if Kanna is coming home for the funeral! It's Auntie Roeslyn's children here. It's Ysie. Hello! Hello!

JIENA

(Wants to take the receiver from YSIE)

Let me try.

*(The receiver is now in the hands of both. Noises.
They look at each other, speechless)*

YSIE

(Hastily)

Goodbye, Kanna. . .

JIENA

Goodbye Kanna. It's Jiena!

MAKIET

(*Who has sat and waited, tensely*)

Ysie, is Kanna coming home, for the funeral? What does he say, Ysie
. . . Jiena. . .?

JIENA

(*Starts to talk, but the words don't come*)

Makiet. . .

> (YSIE *takes* JIENA *by the arm; the two exit, one of them
> still looking back, puzzled.* KANNA *has replaced the receiver.
> He sits alone, also perplexed*)

KANNA

I tried to be tough, the *one* I. Well who was it? Anybody special? That
was the one I. (*Laughs*) 'Is Auntie Roeslyn's children!' That was the
other I. But dammit, who was it? It's from home, from **Your** people.
Didn't you hear? It's from your people. So what did they say? Did
they say something? No, no, I said. You know, after all that they
never say anything. They're not capable of saying anything. No, I said,
no, they only say, Kietie is dead. . .Kietie?. . .Oh yes, I'm sorry, you've
probably forgotten about Kietie. . . So who is Kietie? Our little sister,
I said. And Auntie Roeslyn's children say that Makiet told them to
tell me that Kietie is dead, and if I'm coming home for the funeral.
(*Laughs cynically*)

They must be darned silly people. . . the other I said. O yes, I said,
they're bloody darned silly people. . . I said. . . to expect you to go all
that way for Kietie's funeral. . . Yes, I said. . . and all that money, I said,
but that's just the way they are, I said, so bloody darned silly naive. .
. . As if you could do anything about it. (*Laughs*)

MAKIET

(In another world; again holding out the purse)

Here, Jiena, after all, I've still got my pension for two months, so phone Kanna for me. . . Shame, maybe he won't be able to come, it's very far for him, after all, I mean to come. . . Did he say anything, Jiena *(she smiles silently)* Does he still speak so nicely. . . . Shame, and he's also got mouths to feed. . . How many children has Kanna got now, Jiena?. . . It's so far away, yes. . . What does he say, Ysie, Jiena . . .? *(She smiles)* *(KANNA sits, disturbed)* It's very far away. . . *(Dreamily)* He's gone so very far away from us. . .
*(Noises, announcements, and music, like when one
of the great ocean liners sails)*

KANNA

(Passionately)

I . . . left . . . I couldn't stay, Makiet.

MAKIET

Couldn't you have stayed, Kanna? *(Pause, then dreamily)* Kanna, he went away with the ship. . .
(The ship's warning bells ring, announcements)

KANNA

(Shakes his head slowly, pensively)

No, Makiet, No. *(Silence)*

MAKIET

(Stares straight ahead as if she understands)

No, Kanna couldn't have stayed, I know. . . I know. . .
*(KANNA stands upright, puts his jacket straight, strokes his hair.
A clear sadness over him)*

*(KIETIE, DIEKIE and PANG enter, much younger than before. Shy parting
scenes between KANNA and the three. The props of before are now
moorings on the quay)*

15

MAKIET
(With her blind eyes staring straight ahead over the audience,
smiles sorrowfully)

Goodbye, Kanna!
(She just looks, doesn't wave to him yet. A steam whistle blows.)

(KANNA, upstage, the four—MAKIET, KIETIE, DIEKIE and PANG—form
a group in front. The music stops. A silent waving of hands and
handkerchiefs. A tugboat chugs. KIETIE sobs audibly. Everyone keeps
turning in the direction of the big ship as it maneuvers, until all are
looking out over the audience or the sea. As they turn to the front,
KANNA turns his back while also waving goodbye.
The four in front are a pathetic little group.)

(While all this is happening, they wave, one after the other)

Goodbye, Kanna!

MAKIET
(Tears in her eyes, but strong)

Roeslyn's children came late, but they came, all the same. Shame,
they couldn't just get off from work: they must work hard for their bit
of bread. But they came all the same, because they were also like
brothers and sisters for Kanna: from the time he came to board here
with Roeslyn, when he had to go to the big school here in Cape Town,
before we ourselves came to live here, from the farm. That's how I met
Pang later, too, also through Roeslyn.
(She suddenly laughs happily through the tears)

(YSIE, JIENA, JAKOP, TOEFIE and SKOEN enter and crowd themselves
behind the four as MAKIET talks)

YSIE
(Gestures and shouts)

Kanna, you must write, Kanna, hey!

JIENA

If you need anything, hey Kanna!

MAKIET

Goodbye, Kanna!

> *Everyone silent, waving. Sounds of the sea in Table*
> *Bay, a tugboat, seagulls. Finally everything grows*
> *silent as everyone goes—but* MAKIET, *in her wheel-*
> *chair, still staring, stays.* KANNA *has also stopped*
> *waving. He leans on the ship's railings, his face*
> *towards the back, upstage. The scene remains un-*
> *changed, static, for some time, as only the sounds of*
> *the sea are heard.*

(Music)

3. It's Kietie ——————————————————————

(The music changes to the cry of a single seagull.)

MAKIET

(Staring out)

Yes, we said, look, Kanna is very clever, Kanna he's got such a good head, he's going to become a great man here, among our people. Then we're going to live better, yes, because we're living a hard life, we live very hard. . . We know we haven't got privileges like . . . the white people. . .

(Neon lights flicker. Cash registers jingling in a shop)

VOICE

*(A woman's—as if attending to someone, syrupy.
It is the white saleslady, serving a white customer.)*

(MAKIET listens)

Yes ma'am. You been served already, ma'am? Can I help you? *(Pause)* Oh yes, sure, ma'am, come see over here, would you, ma'am. . . Yes, it's just darling, isn't it. . .

MAKIET

(Dreamily)

It was about every six months or so that Kietie and me, we went into Cape Town, to the big bazaar for a bit of clothes. The ladies behind the counter spoke English, it was difficult for us. . . But Kietie was always so crazy over the georgette.

(Laughs her little laugh) (Pause)

VOICE

(Gruffly)

Yes, what is it you want! Georgette?

MAKIET

We lived very hard. . . .

VOICE

Yes, just go and look over there, will you?
>*(Jingle of cash registers, the voice growing impatient)*

Yes, yes, I'm coming. I'm just serving the lady here. . .
>*(Aside, and in a friendly tone)*

Oh, sorry, ma'am. *(Laughs shyly)*

MAKIET

Oh, well. . . The georgette was the latest fashion then. . .
>*(Pause)*

It's been a long time. . .
>*(MAKIET sits pensive and listening. In thought,*
>*her hand moves over the chair's edge)*

It's been a long time. Shame, poor Roeslyn.
>*(Smiles)*

Roeslyn, her kitchen was always a lovely little place.
>*(ROESLYN enters. She's of the stout and busy sort. She starts to take*
>*imaginary washing down from an imaginary clothesline, carries the*
>*bundle in her arms into the imaginary kitchen, and puts it*
>*down on a chair. Then she begins to busy herself in the kitchen.*
>*Puts irons on one side of the old coal stove, washes dishes,*
>*sweeps, stokes the stove, and so on)*

>*(MAKIET laughs a little when she speaks again, pouts a little,*
>*her hand moving on the chair's edge)*

She was always so busy, she made the fire like so, she set up the irons like so, she sprinkled the washing to dampen it like so, she always bustled about like so. . . *(Pause)* She kneaded bread like so . . . *(Laughs)*

ROESLYN

Kietie!

KIETIE

(*Offstage*)

Auntie Roeslyn?
(*She enters, walking with a slight but noticeable limp*)

MAKIET

Yes, the georgette was the latest then.

ROESLYN

Cut a few patterns for the kitchen dresser's shelves.

KIETIE

Yes, Auntie.

ROESLYN

There's some old papers under the chesterfield, in the lounge. . .
(KIETIE *moves a little, then bends down looking
under the imaginary couch*)

MAKIET

(*Dreamily*)

He's coming home. He did say he was going to come again. I'll be back
very soon, Makiet, he said. . . (*Smiles*)

ROESLYN

Diekie!

(DIEKIE *enters*)

DIEKIE

Did Mama call for me?

ROESLYN

Yes, go get some lamp oil at the shop, quick, and a brown bread. Hurry up!

KIETIE

Under the chesterfield, Auntie Roeslyn? There's then nothing here!
(DIEKIE *takes the money and bottles, exits*)

ROESLYN
(*After him*)

Hurry up, hey!
(*To* KIETIE)

Under the seat, look under the seat, my dear. . .
(*After a while*)

Did you get it?

KIETIE

Yes, Auntie.

(*She moves to the kitchen*)

ROESLYN
(*Busy at the stove*)

No, we won't see him again, I said to your Mommy, Kietie, not the way I know our Kanna. Our Kanna he's got such a good head, the people over there they're going to keep him there. . . and Kanna, his heart wasn't really here, either. . .

MAKIET
(*Decisively*)

No! He said himself he was coming again to us, so he'll be coming again, to us.

21

KIETIE

(*Searching in the drawers of the kitchen cupboard*)

Where's the scissors, Auntie Roesyln?

ROESLYN

They should be there in the drawer, my child.

KIETIE

(*Has found the scissors*)

Okay, Auntie. I'll go work in the hall.
(*She moves aside as* ROESLYN *looks after her*)

ROESLYN

Shame, I almost said the wrong thing, now. I almost said, Why's your leg so bad again today, my dear?. . . Shame. . .
(*Shakes her head*)

Too bad!

(*She sighs*)

MAKIET

He'll come again to us, Roeslyn!

ROESLYN

But such is life, I always say, 'coz what else can a person say?

KIETIE

It doesn't matter any more, Auntie.

ECHO

(*Ominously*)

It doesn't matter any more. . .

MAKIET
(*Excited*)

Keep quiet, yes. . .

ECHO

Quiet. . .

(*A pause*)

MAKIET

Or they'll kill us all, so keep quiet. . .

ECHO

(*Softly*)
Or they'll kill us all. . .
(*A gasping fills the hall. Then the terrible sounds from outside, a little
girl screaming. ROESLYN stiffens up, imaginary dough in her hands, for
she was just then kneading bread, and MAKIET, anxious in her chair.
They rush over to the kitchen window. KIETIE, the adult KIETIE, stays
put on stage, head buried in her lap. For long, intense moments,
MAKIET and ROESLYN peer speechlessly, dumbly, out the window,
until MAKIET speaks*)

MAKIET
(*Helplessly, but strong even now*)

Roeslyn! Roeslyn! It's Kietie, Roeslyn!
(*ROESLYN cries; tears standing in her shocked eyes.
Oblivious to her surroundings*)

ROESLYN

It's Kietie!

23

MAKIET

(*Overwhelmed, but strong*)

It's Kietie!

KIETIE

(*The adult* KIETIE)

But it doesn't matter any more now.

MAKIET

It's Kietie!
>(*As if in pain, she feels her leg, and looks at it while
>she raises her skirt; she lets it fall again*)

DIEKIE

(*Pulls away suddenly, clenches his fists angrily in the air*)

They're pigs, Mamma! They're rubbish, the swine!
>(*Then he cries inconsolably in* MAKIET'S *lap*)

Pigs! Pigs! I'll kill them, still. . .

MAKIET

(*Puts her hands through his hair*)

Diekie, my child! Diekie! Diekie! Diekie, my child!
(*Then, irregular little footsteps.* ROESLYN *and* MAKIET *hear them, tense
up, and stare at the kitchen door. Besides the footsteps, also a gasping.
Then a fishhorn blows, it's a dejected sound, a message that it
really doesn't matter, and that life goes on.*

Then she appears, little KIETIE, *in the kitchen door. A little girl of seven
who has just been raped. She clutches the door frame, her eyes are
glassy, her mouth moving like a dying little fish's, a vision of
terror fulfilled.*

*For a moment she stares, panting, beside the kitchen door. Then she
moves in, closer. In horror, she comes closer, touching the household*

24

things. Limping. Everyone stares now, just stares,
even little DIEKIE, *at the vision.)*

KIETIE

(The raped little girl, staring and gasping and approaching closer)
Makiet!
(And it is as if everyone around fears her. Except Makiet)

MAKIET

(Whispering, passionately)
Kietie, it's you! My child, my Kietie! My Kietie!
(The fishhorn sounding at a distance. The last light shines
on little KIETIE, *analyzing and showing all.)*
(Then dim, and in this dim light, KIETIE *falls into the old woman's lap.)*

KIETIE

Makiet. . .

ROESLYN

We must phone the police. . .

MAKIET

(Immediately)
No! They'll kill you! . . . they'll kill us all!
(Then DIEKIE *bursts in, dazed)*

DIEKIE

Makiet! Auntie Roeslyn! They've caught Kietie!
(He cries loudly as the women remain dumb,
apparently neither of them conscious of him.)

Auntie Roeslyn! Makiet! They caught Kietie!
> (*At last* ROESLYN *notices him*) (*Through tears,*
> *his words coming quickly*)

They caught Kietie! Listen! They grabbed her, they just grabbed her,
then they dragged her into the alley, Makiet,
> (*He is close enough for* ROESLYN *to squeeze his mouth shut*)

ROESLYN

All right, Diekie, all right! Now be quiet and shut up, and go and
stand there by Makiet!
> (*He comes to stand by* MAKIET)

DIEKIE
(*Sobs*)

. . . Then . . . they. . .

ROESLYN
(*Shouts*)

Didn't I tell you, Diekie, to shut up!? Didn't I!?
> (DIEKIE *just stands there and sobs beside* MAKIET
> (*who puts her arms around him.*)

MAKIET

Diekie, my child. . . Diekie. . .
> (*then whispering*)

Kietie.

KIETIE
(*the adult* KIETIE)

But I said it doesn't make any difference any more.

MAKIET

Kietie, my child . . .
  (*Caresses little* KIETIE, *embraces her lovingly, as the others just stare*)

  Blackout

  Fishhorn

4. So They Put Their Things on the Little Cart ———

When the lights come up, KANNA and MAKIET on stage. KANNA upstage, smoking, his face towards the audience. MAKIET, in her chair, is right front on stage, gazing out. In the distance, the fishhorn blows. KANNA puts out his cigarette. Then the sharp cry of the single seagull.

KANNA

(Sitting on the rail)

Poverty and the evil of it,
Day in, day out.
Year in, year out, the indignity.
Generation upon generation.

(He imitates MAKIET)

But God, He is really also full of mercy! *(Laughs)*

(KANNA falls silent, an air of bitterness upon him)

Kanna doesn't answer. He lives far away now. He isn't coming back. Roeslyn, she was right. Yes, Roeslyn, she was right.

KANNA

(Softly, aside)

Come back?

MAKIET

He should have come back . . .

KANNA

(Softly)

Where to?

MAKIET

. . . To us. . . to your people

KANNA

(*Does not speak*)

MAKIET

Then we would have lived better by now.

KANNA

Poor Makiet!

MAKIET

We brought him up—it was hard, for him. . . for us. . .

KANNA

Makiet!

MAKIET

. . . First Paans and me, on the farm, then me and Pang, here in Cape Town . . .

KANNA

Do you know what the Bible says, Makiet?

MAKIET

Yes, we brought him up, it was very hard. . .
(KANNA *makes a gesture of despair*) . . . so it breaks our hearts now that he stays so far away. Yes, I know Kanna wasn't the child of our own flesh, but our adopted child. But he wasn't a throwaway child. Never. No, we brought him up, caring, just like all our other children, like Kietie, and like Diekie, first Paans and me, and then later me and Pang. We brought them up, the same, all. . .

KANNA

Makiet, the Bible says. . .

MAKIET

(She gives her little laugh)

See these little old hands? *(Holds up her hands)*
They're cracked this way from all the hard work. It was hard work. It
was very hard work. Sometimes I couldn't hold out the whole day, and
the children they also wanted to see me at home sometimes.

KANNA

We'll have the poor with us always, Makiet!
(MAKIET laughs her little laugh, then listens attentively. KANNA too)

WOMAN'S VOICE

*(Calls, somewhat at a distance. It is the white madam
of MAKIET'S younger years)*

Katie, K-a-t-i-e! -ie! ie!
(Pause, then again)

K-a-a-t-i-e!
(Pause, then with irritation)

Now didn't the girl come in this morning? Again? How much trouble
a person has with these . . . people.
(Spitting out the word. Then, even angrier)

How much trouble with these people . . . What do I do, now! Ship
out the kids again today, shame, the poor darlings . . .
*(There is dejection in KANNA'S eyes. He gazes out silently before him.
A long silence. At last MAKIET gives her little laugh)*

MAKIET

You were saying something about the Bible, Kanna?
(KANNA does not speak)

MAKIET

(*Louder*) What did you say about the Bible?
(KANNA *sits dejectedly. He does not answer.*
The fishhorn blasts in the distance)

KANNA

(At *last, dreamily*)

They adopted me, took me in from a home for orphan kids.
I grew up. . .

MAKIET

. . . with us, first with me and Paans, and then with me
and Pang. . .

KANNA

Yes.

MAKIET

. . . just like our very own children. Just like Kietie and Diekie . . .

KANNA

I loved them. I loved them . . .

MAKIET

. . . First me and Paans, and then me and Pang, and Kietie
and Diekie. . .

KANNA

. . . And Auntie Roeslyn and Auntie Roeslyn's children and . . .

MAKIET

. . . us all . . . (*silence*)

KANNA

I went to school.

MAKIET

. . . first on the farm . . .

KANNA

. . . on Makiet's char money, her payment for washing other people's clothes. . .

MAKIET

. . . Together with Kietie and Diekie. . .

KANNA

. . . on Makiet's char money. . .

MAKIET

The welfare money was also a help. . . Me and Paans, that time, we thought, well, Kanna, he's so clever, the school teachers said so too, so let's give him the very best that we can. No, no, no. He wasn't a throwaway child. Not even a little bit. Shame, poor Paans, he couldn't actually work anymore, the TB does that. . .

KANNA

The TB. . .

MAKIET

The TB, yes. Shame, Paans is already under the earth all these years, him and little Krools. He coughed blood so, that's what the TB does . . .

KANNA

The TB.

MAKIET

The drinking . . . but that wasn't a good word. The doctor said it was from drinking . . . it's from the wine, he said . . . Paans, he also tried his best. He wasn't really bad to me . . . I look like I look now mostly from all the hard years of work in the hot sun. And even before then, well, when we were just recently married, just the riding around from place to place in the cart. Paans, he still had the first donkeys then, and we just rode through the Karoo, just rode around, in circles, really. But those were wonderful days, actually. (*She gives her little laugh*) Many times, right there, in the veld, under the low bushes in the veld. (*Laughs*) Paans was also a wild one in his day.

(MAKIET *laughs again*)

But when he saw little Krools was coming, he said to me: No, Kieta, now we *must* find a place. A standing place. So actually he was very good to me. (*Pause*) Then Paans died, on the farm. (*Her hand moves again on the chair*) Then Paans died. . .

KANNA

(*Quickly*) I was already boarding, in Cape Town.

MAKIET

So we also went, what else was there for us to do on the farm. . .

KANNA

So we also went, what else was there for us to do on the farm. . .
. . . the **baas** also said so. . . (*Bitter laughter*)

MAKIET

. . . the boss farmer, yes. (*Pause*) So, we put our things on the little cart. . . (*Silence*)

KANNA

(*Aside*) So, they just put their things on the little cart. . .
(*Silence*) (*With empathy, looking at* MAKIET)

Shame, Makiet!

(He comes forward, stands behind her chair, takes her head in his
hands, strokes her hair, moved)

Makiet!

(MAKIET, also emotional. Her hands search behind her, find KANNA'S,
hold them) (they remain in this position for some time)

(Smiles) Then Paans died, then you just put our things on the little
cart, Makiet?

(MAKIET stares)   (Again they hold the position for some time.
Then they listen to the sounds of the donkey cart going
on the highway. It fills the hall)

Can you imagine that road? The donkey cart, and the few household
things, and the one donkey, and little Diekie with the reins, and
Makiet with the reins, and little Kietie. . .

(He bends his arms as if holding reins. Now DIEKIE appears, playing a
boy of nine. Excited. His arms bent for the journey, he clicks his tongue
like a horse's trot as he jogs forward after making some wide turns
across the stage, and takes the reins from KANNA. They look at each
other as if there is a knowing understanding between them. KANNA
nods at DIEKIE and moves aside, from where he observes the journey,
and speaks. Now and then DIEKIE acts as if he himself is the donkey,
JAPIE, and MAKIET'S chair the cart, then again, he pushes his hands
backwards, grips the back of the chair and acts as if he is riding in the
cart with MAKIET and KIETIE. KANNA participates in all of this)

KANNA

Ride him, Diekie!

DIEKIE

Come on, Japie-donkey, come, come. . .
Pappa Paans is dead, Japie-donkey. Come on now to Cape Town, let's
see how life is there . . . then we'll be near Kanna, too . . . Come on,
Japie.

(Sounds of the cart in the distance. KANNA speaks above it)

KANNA

From where that little cart came? From where Paans came? (*Laughs*)
I always say the Bible is a wonderful book! There are answers for you!
(*Laughs, then speaks loudly*) "God said: Let us create man in our image,
in our likeness . . . And the Lord God formed man out of the dust of
the earth. . ." Out of the dust! That's where they all come from! Yes!
(KANNA's *cynical laughter echoes through the hall. When it dies away,
the sounds of the cart are heard again*)

DIEKIE

Can you see the city lights, Japie-donkey? (*Pause*) Just look at the
people in their motor-cars staring at us! That's where Kanna is staying
wit Auntie Roeslyn, and Jakop and Toefie, and Skoen, and Ysie, and
Jiena. . . (*he points*) (*The donkey trots more slowly*)

KANNA

Look at the people staring, Diekie!

DIEKIE

Japie, it's a little steep now, be careful. Yes, I know these round old
stones are a nuisance, a shame, but that's the way they made some of
the roads around here. Japie. . .
(*The wheels roll slowly and unrhythmically over the cobblestones*)

MAKIET

(*Who has recovered, excitedly*)

Just *two* more streets, Diekie. Auntie Roeslyn, she lives on Blom
Street!

JAPIE (DIEKIE)

Yes, Mamma. Mamma?. . .

DIEKIE

(*He acts as if dragging the cart forward*)

He's tired, Mama. . .

MAKIET

For shame, Japie. He's also come a long way. . . . come on, Japie!
(She laughs a little)

DIEKIE

(*Bends his arms for* JAPIE, *then for* MAKIET) We're really riding now!
(*He laughs, his arms bent*) (MAKIET *responds, also bending her arms*)

KANNA

(*Warning*) Look at the people staring, Diekie!

DIEKIE

Come on, Japie!

MAKIET AND DIEKIE

(*Laughing together*)

Come on, Japie! Just *one* more street! Auntie Roeslyn, she lives on
Blom Street!

DIEKIE

Yes, Mamma!

(*They're riding now*) (*Holds out his hand*)

There, give him the whip, Mamma!
(MAKIET *does not take the whip, but looks up laughingly at* DIEKIE)

KANNA

Diekie. . .

(MAKIET *and* DIEKIE *laugh. But the laughter freezes,*
and the moment after, they stare)

MAKIET

Look how the people are staring at us, Diekie!

DIEKIE

(*The expression on his face has changed, he gnashes his teeth,
purses his lips*)

Just one more street, Mamma.
(*Mocking noises*)

(*Half over his shoulder*)

Don't look at them, Kietie! Sit right back in there! Don't look at
them! (*He hisses through his teeth*) The bastards!

(*To* MAKIET)

What's so funny about us? Just this next turn still, Ma. . .

MAKIET

(*Upset*) It's not nice here, Diekie. . .

(*But suddenly, transported to another world*)

There's Kanna! Look, there's Kanna!

(*She waves excitedly*) (KANNA *stands towards the back,
in the shadows upstage*)

DIEKIE

There's Auntie Roeslyn!

(*He waves.* ROESLYN, YSIE, JIENA, TOEFIE, *and* SKOEN
enter on one side. They wave and laugh)

ROESLYN AND THE OTHERS

It's Makiet and them! Hello, Kiet! Haai, Diekie! Haai!

DIEKIE

Haai, Toefie! Haai, Skoen!

MAKIET

Kanna!

(*Then, her face twisting, she speaks in dismay*)

Why... doesn't Kanna wave to us, Diekie? Why doesn't Kanna wave? (*Pause*) Diekie, why doesn't Kanna... wave?
(*Silence*)

(*Finally* KANNA *speaks from the shadows. He is barely visible, his voice a hollow sound*)

KANNA

(*Frustrated, bitter*)

Kanna didn't wave because... because... Say anything at all. Say what you will! But you can't say Kanna didn't wave because Kanna didn't love you! No, you can't say *that*!

5. The Oracle of God

The stage remains largely unchanged, only everyone remains motionless as Kanna speaks again.

KANNA

(He has changed his manner, to one of aggression, and appears in the light)

I will tell! I will tell! That first summer they. . . caught Kietie, like Diekie said. They. . . raped Kietie! In broad daylight, on the street! (*The fisherhorn sounds*) Can you hear? (*Then a girl's muffled scream in the distance*) Do you hear?

(MAKIET has turned her chair in the direction everyone is looking, and they all stare)

God knows how many people there were looking on. Jakop of Roeslyn was already a grown man and he pushed me back into the house. Toefie and Skoen were mad, upset! Diekie hysterical. But Jakop was strong. Jakop was then a preacher of some sort or other, like Diekie later. Many a day he stood on the Parade, talking at the people! Preaching! So Jakop said, it's no use, he said, it will just cause bloodshed to retaliate, you're just looking for your own deaths too! I'm telling you, stay inside the house! (*Imitates* JAKOP) It's no use, unless they decide to change themselves, to get converted! I remember how I detested Jakop then. And Diekie! (*Laughs and imitates* DIEKIE) You're a fuckin' coward, Diekie said to him.

DIEKIE

You're a fuckin' coward!

(KANNA laughs)

(Sounds of panting and footsteps. Everyone stares at the kitchen door. Then KIETIE appears. The scene is like the previous one, except that everyone is silent and they just stare. This time she also does not come to the front of the stage, showing the vision of herself for just a moment in the kitchen door, then exits.)

(Everyone, except KANNA, moves curiously and fearfully to the kitchen door, after KIETIE; then everyone but ROESLYN and MAKIET off as KANNA starts talking again)

KANNA

There was the other time.
> (MAKIET *and* ROESLYN *swing around in dismay.*
> *They speak simultaneously*)

Kanna!

MAKIET

Kanna, no!

ROESLYN

No! You can't tell!

KANNA

(BRUSQUELY)

I'm already telling.
> (*While he is speaking,* KIETIE—*the adult* KIETIE—*appears on stage.*
> *She observes all, silently*)

KIETIE

Please Kanna!

MAKIET
(*Half-hysterical*)

You must not tell! It's . . . too much. . . it's. . .

ROESLYN
(*Agitated*)

We're not so bad, Kanna! You can't say we're so bad. . .

KANNA
(*Determined*)

There was the other time.
> (*They come closer. He disentangles himself from them.*
> *The scene is now center stage*)

KANNA

Leave me alone!
> (*Silence*) (*The three remain near him, fear-stricken*) (*Aside*)

"Who is there amongst you that, when his son asks for bread, will give him a stone; and when he asks for fish, will give him a snake? If you who are bad know how to do good favors for your children how much more will your Father who is in heaven. . ."
> (*Here his words are drowned out by the band*
> *that starts playing: "Come let us sing!"*)

> (JAKOP *in. With arms outstretched, and large in his presence,*
> *he walks through the little group, enraptured, as if preaching on one*
> *of the street corners. He speaks the words of "Come let us sing,"*
> *in time with the music!*)

JAKOP

Friends,
Let us open the Bible
And read from it. . .

KANNA

Yes, Jakop still believed, then. . .

JAKOP

Oh, Almighty Spirit
Let these words go to our hearts!. . .

41

KANNA

Jakop believed in God. . .

JAKOP

. . . From the second book of Moses, Exodus, from the fourth chapter, the first and the second verses. . .
(*Everyone listens now*)

KANNA

Jakop prayed.

JAKOP

O God,
Make light with these words for us, like candles!
Jakop prayed for the people.
(*A crowd gathers round* JAKOP. *Together with the crowd and the audience,* JAKOP *is now encircled by a multitude for whom he preaches. He speaks to them, to God, to himself.*)

JAKOP

Then Moses answered and said: But what if they don't believe me, don't take hold of my words, if they say the Lord didn't appear to me?

KANNA

Some of them listened, others laughed.

JAKOP

But the Lord said to him, You will lead your people.
What is in your hand?
and Moses said: A Staff. . .

KANNA

"I am the Oracle of God," Jakop told them,
"I am the Oracle of God!"

JAKOP

(*Gestures*)

Now friends,
That was all that he had
this man of God,
a staff
a stick, just a dead stick,
and on top of it all, he also stuttered, he couldn't speak. . .

KANNA

(*Agitated himself*)

Jakop prayed for salvation for the people!

JAKOP

But the Lord then spoke with him, for a long time, about how he had
killed the Egyptian with that stick, and Moses hung his head, that
great big head. . .
And then, and then
suddenly that selfsame stick
in his hand was a snake!

KANNA

Jakop prayed for bread for the people!

JAKOP

Now friends,
The Lord has wrought His miracle
with me also, like this
He asked me what was in my hand
and friends there in my hand, I saw, was my guitar. . .
Come, let us sing!!
(*Totally enraptured,* JAKOP *begins to sing. The people closest
to him in the crowd start singing with him, then others too, till
all are singing, and it fills the hall. The bodies sway and the hands
clap as* JAKOP *leads them on*)

43

(The dialogue continues in the momentary lulls of this singing)

KANNA

"I am the Oracle of God," Jakop said to them.

JAKOP

I am the Oracle of God!

KANNA

"God speaks, listen," Jakop told them.

JAKOP

Friends, God speaks, listen! Listen!

KANNA

God is merciful, listen.

JAKOP

The Lord, He's merciful, listen! Friends, listen!

KANNA

God is good.

JAKOP

The Lord, He's very good! Don't you believe me, then?

KANNA

God gives us bread!

JAKOP
(Prays)

Our Father
Who is up in Heaven,

Your name is Holy!
Your Kingdom come,
Your will be done
on the earth
just like it is in Heaven there above!
Give us today our daily bread, please.

CROWD

Halleluja!

JAKOP

Halleluja!
Amen! Amen!
(*The music and song stop momentarily. All freeze in their positions.*
JAKOP, *with raised arms, stares out over the audience.* KANNA
starts talking, while also motionless.)

MAKIET

(*Sits absolutely still, staring straight ahead*)

No, we shouldn't have told. . .

ROESLYN

We really shouldn't have. . .

KIETIE

(*Breaking into the scene*)

But it doesn't matter any more, so you can just tell. . .

KANNA

(*Motionless. His first words overlap her last*)

That was the first time we knew Kietie and Jakop were . . . in love.

JAKOP

(*He doesn't move, only looks up, heavenward*)

Kietie!

KIETIE

Ja, Jakop!

KANNA

It was an evening after one of Jakop's street sermons. Kietie was then working "in service," as they say. She was "sleeping in," as they say. But it was, as they say, her "weekend off." She was on her way home. Jakop was going to meet her halfway, they had arranged where he would meet her. (*Then he speaks with more pace*) Jakop was on his way there. He was walking. . . He was thinking of Kietie, how he always said her name, how they would talk with each other. He was thinking of her as he walked towards where he would meet her. In his mind he heard how they spoke to each other, always, and how pretty her voice always rings when she said, "Ja, Jakop."

(*Footsteps*) (*Kietie and Jakop join each other, center stage*)

JAKOP

Kietie. . .

KIETIE

Ja, Jakop.

JAKOP

(*Tenderly*)

They must have faith. That's the only thing that I can see for them, I mean the people. . .

KIETIE

Ja, Jakop.

JAKOP

The Lord, He will be good for them, but they have to mend their ways.

KIETIE

Ja, Jakop.

JAKOP

Kietie!

KIETIE

Ja, Jakop?

JAKOP

The Lord is merciful. Do you believe that?

KIETIE

Ja, Jakop.

(*Silence*)

JAKOP

How was it at work this week, Kietie?

KIETIE

No, it was good, Jakop. . .

JAKOP

Kietie. . .

KIETIE

Ja, Jakop.

JAKOP

The Lord, He's good. Do you really believe it?

47

KIETIE

Yes, I believe it, Jakop. I believe. . .

KANNA

When he arrived there, at the appointed place, he could not find her.
He searched for her. But he was sensing what had happened.
(*Suddenly she is gasping. The scene shifts back to reality.
She tries to shake off the cruel hands that smother her,
struggling and screaming. The footsteps have become the
sound of someone madly running.* JAKOP *has come to life*)

JAKOP

(*Stares out before him, he calls*)

Kietie! (*To his left*)
Kietie! (*To his right*)
Kietie! Kietie! (*All over*) Kietie! Kietie!
(*Has turned around. Bursts through the crowd, his crazed words
pouring from his throat, overlapping* ROESLYN *and* MAKIET)

Kietie! Have you seen Kietie? I mean Kietie!
Have you seen Kietie?

MAKIET

We shouldn't have told. . .

JAKOP

A young girl. . .

ROESLYN

We rather shouldn't have. . .

JAKOP

She was coming home from work . . . Innocently.

MAKIET

We mustn't tell. . .

JAKOP

Kietie. . .

KANNA

By this time Jakop knew clearly what had happened.

JAKOP

Have you . . . seen . . .

KANNA

Then he saw, for the second time, in his life, he saw. . . How they had
. . .

(JAKOP *comes to a dumbfounded halt on the stage.*
MAKIET *faints in her chair*)

VOICES

The old woman! Over here! Help the old woman!
(ROESLYN *and one or two of the others range themselves
beside* MAKIET *to help her*)

JAKOP
(*Stares out toward the back*)

Kietie!
(*He falls on his knees*)

Kietie!
(KIETIE *herself, on stage, looks out bewildered for a moment.
Then she sobs, she cries hysterically.* JAKOP, *protecting,
but too late, falls over her*)

KANNA

Jakop was strong. But the shock of Kietie, his Kietie, big Kietie, ravaged another time—it took half his strength. He tried to protect her, he was strong, but there were five, six, seven of them, thugs, seven against him alone, against Jakop, and the shock . . . People, the police, it doesn't matter who, brought him home that night, carried him in. Poor Jakop . . . Jakop . . . He had put up one hell of a fight . . . he who didn't believe in violence . . . (*silence*)

When Kietie didn't show up for work the next week, the white madam, as they say, came to look for her. They told her what had happened. She drove away, the white madam, in her big car. Oh, these people, she said, and shook her head. Oh, these people.

(*Laughs*)

(*Silence*)

No, Jakop did not preach again. He lay in bed, he talked deliriously, in a coma, months on end . . .

(*Silence*)

Jakop did not believe in violence. Remember how he shoved us back into the house, that first time. You're just looking for your own death, it's no use unless they change and convert themselves! This time it was different. Kietie meant something different to him than that first time . . .

(*Silence, ominously*)

And then Jakop heard. . .

MAKIET
(*Who has recovered, faintly*)

No! No!

ROESLYN
(*Screaming*)

No!!

KANNA
. . . Kietie was going to have a child, from the rape!

JAKOP
(*On the floor, behind them, a dumb, animal-like sound about his voice*)
Kietie! Kietie!

KANNA
Roeslyn. . .

MAKIET
No! No! Oh, my God. . .

ROESLYN
(*Stiffens beside* MAKIET'S *chair, dismayed*)
No!

KANNA
. . . Roeslyn tried an abortion. . .

JAKOP
Kietie!
(KIETIE *laughs crazily*)

KANNA
We found Jakop in his bed, that morning. . .

JAKOP
(*Ruckling*)
Kietie. . .

51

KANNA

. . .in that purple-red bed. . .
> (*The fishhorn in the distance*)

No, Jakop did not preach again.
> (*The fishhorn*)

The oracle of God did not preach again. . . He was dead. . . in that purple-red bed. . . the blood. . .

> (KIETIE *laughs shrilly. Her laughter mocks everyone,
> as it echoes through the hall. She's mad.*)

> (*The crowd disperses towards the back, staring.
> The southeaster starts blowing.*)

KANNA

Things happened as they had to, and then came the night that Kietie dug out an old Christmas card, from a cupboard drawer. God knows what she thought, whether it was a symbol of sorts. . . She tied it round the miserable little creature's neck, and she went out and let it loose in the dark night. That's how they found it, the way the newspapers described it, anyway. . . It was quite a story for them. (*Laughs*)

> *There is the echo of* KIETIE'S *laughter. Then only the
> wind blows.* KANNA *moves upstage, where he kneels
> beside* JAKOP'S *body, his fingers running through the
> dead* JAKOP'S *hair. The stage grows dark except for
> the light around* JAKOP, *and* KANNA *over him.*

> *Fade out to the sound of boisterous Cape Town music.*

6. Goodbye, Diekie

The guitars take over. It is music of a kind to make people tap their feet without consciously wanting to. Lights slowly up. KANNA *and* MAKIET *on stage.* TOEFIE *and* SKOEN *are busy setting up the scene: an elemental double-storey structure in a poor neighborhood, somewhat dilapidated and overcrowded.*

The audience sees the front section of this building. The ground floor shows a small shop with porch in front. The shutters of the display window are sealed up. The floor above shows the outside wall of a bedroom with two small windows. As yet no light in these windows.

To the left, the breadth of a street slopes upstage. In the corner the wall forms with the street is a door of the little shop with the sealed-up shutters. To the right, also sloping upstage, is a dark alley.

TOEFIE *and* SKOEN *have already been busy for some time before* MAKIET *speaks.* KANNA *has been watching them with interest, and has helped them here and there.*

MAKIET
(Who remains staring out over the audience)

What are they doing, Kanna?

KANNA
(Busy with TOEFIE *and* SKOEN, *inspecting the structure)*

It's Pang's place, like it was, Makiet, the little shop, and on top. . . upstairs. . . (*He laughs a little*) And Boela's fish shop down there. (*He indicates the street*)

MAKIET

Shame, poor Pang.
(*Two* GUITAR PLAYERS *on. They had made the music earlier, but now have stopped playing. They sit themselves down on the shop's porch, towards the front, one of them still plucking at the guitar strings. The other has begun smoking.*)

(*Front stage,* MAKIET *in her chair*)

MAKIET

Yes, it was all those things that broke Pang's heart. All those things. He was never very healthy, and he was a very good man, my second husband. (*A pause. Then dreamily*)
Too bad, poor Kietie.

KANNA

Kietie was never in her right mind again, I heard.

MAKIET

But she tried to carry on. She tried to be good. No, she was not like other girls, and she made much of Jakop just because Jakop preached. (*A pause. Then again broodingly*) Shame, poor Pang.

KANNA

Pang was good to me, very good.
(*Then lights appear in the windows upstairs.* KANNA *looks up.* MAKIET *too. Then* PANG'S *coughing is heard from above, an ugly cough, and long*)

MAKIET

(*Again she looks out over the audience*)

Bai took over the little shop for Pang. (*Pause*) No, Pang never got up again, from his bed, I mean . . .

(The scene is at last completely set up, and TOEFIE *and* SKOEN *exit.* BAI, *thin and gray, enters right, a bunch of keys dangling in his hands. As he passes the* GUITAR PLAYERS *on the porch, they greet him without looking up)*

TOEFIE AND SKOEN

Hey, Bai! hey Bai!

BAI

(His voice rasping)

Hey, Toefie! Hey, Skoen!
(He unlocks the door and disappears into the little shop, then again the coughing)

KANNA

It was Pang who let me study further, as they say.

MAKIET

So Pang also felt very bad when Kanna left us like that. Yes, he really felt bad.

(Silence)

*(*KANNA *diagonally behind* MAKIET, *his manner tense. He looks up at the windows again. The* GUITAR PLAYERS *plucking their strings a little. Enter* SONNY, *the fruit peddler, pushing his imaginary hawker's cart before him, moving up to the corner of the porch, all the time arranging his wares, shining them up, and so on. Enter also the* FLOWER SELLER, *with an imaginary batch of flowers on her head, which she puts down immediately, to broadcast her wares even before she sits beside it, shaking the flower bunches.)*

FLOWER SELLER

Carnations!
Red carnations!
White carnations!

SONNY

Hell, you can hold the funeral later, you little bitch!

FLOWER SELLER

Go on and fuck off, you with your dead bananas. Go, little bitch, to
your mother!

SONNY

Hell, how do you know about my dead bananas!?
(*Laughs*)

And I've got no mother, man! I'm just my own person!
(*Then* BOELA *on—it is he who has the little fish shop down the street.
Like* BAI, *he is gray, but unlike the skinny* BAI, BOELA *has a large, hairy
chest that shows through the buttons of his shirt, and his belly is large.
Despite his asthma and his snoring, a cigarette hangs from his lips all
the time, even when he speaks. And like* BAI, *he wears suspenders.* BAI
also on the porch now, in front of the shop door.)

MAKIET

Yes, after Pang died, Kietie just went and married the terrible Poena.
Diekie was against it and so were all of us.
(DIEKIE—*the grown* DIEKIE—*enters left, upset and confused, gesticulat-
ing*)

DIEKIE

But Ma, how can Kietie. . . Kietie! Is she going to marry. . . Poena!?
Marry! Marry!? Poena!? (*Helplessly*)
But he's a bastard, he's. . . rubbish, I tell you, Ma.
(*At his wits' end*)

Doesn't she see what's already happened!?

(*A pause*)

Did she forget Jakop, then?

(*He realizes what he has said and finally comes to stand diagonally*

across from MAKIET *and* KANNA. *Then as if he reports to* KANNA,
softly)

Kanna, Poena, he was rubbish, real rubbish, a swine! You know, no,
you won't know, but I was converted. Jakop did it for me. No, you
wouldn't know. But I was born again, then that pig broke my
conversion again. . .

KANNA

Diekie didn't forget Jakop. Also not that day Kietie was seven years
old. And Diekie didn't want it to happen again. Not on his life!

DIEKIE

'Is true, Kanna, what I say. He was a real swine! You would have said
so too, if you were only here, Kanna! but you weren't here.

MAKIET
(Echoes the words)

If Kanna was only here . . .

KANNA

Quiet! Not again!

DIEKIE

But Kanna. . .

FLOWER SELLER
(Monotonously)

Carnations!
Red carnations!
White carnations!
Carnations!

MAKIET

Ttoo bad; poor Kietie.
  (*The one* GUITAR PLAYER *plucking the strings in a lively manner.*
  But when PANG *coughs in the room above, he stops*)

MAKIET

We were still living in the heart of town, then, in District Six.

SONNY

(*To the* GUITAR PLAYER)

Hey, I say, pal, sing some blues, man! How can you be so happy, happy with the business so bad, hey? I've been standing here the whole day so far in this shit heat, for bloody nothing!
  (*Then he shouts in all directions*)

Tomatoes! Tomatoes! Potatoes, fresh potatoes, for free, just four pence a pound, and no joking!
(*He laughs*) (*The* GUITAR PLAYERS *don't answer. Everyone just silent.*
  SONNY *does not yet see* BOELA *walking up to him*)

BAI

(*Who sees* BOELA *approaching, raspingly*)

You can speak a little softer, Sonny, man. . .
  (SONNY, *in his mood, doesn't look up from his fruit.*
  He pulls a face, and carries on)

SONNY

Hey, what smells so bad, hey? Must be old Boela's fish stinking down there? (*He laughs*)
  (BOELA *is close by, now. He speaks with the leisurely authority*
  that is his in the district)

BOELA

Sonny, listen, you talk too much. Too bloody much, I say. Doesn't

that jaw of yours ever get tired, man? Old Pang is lying sick up there, and don't you have the first bit of respect then, man. . .
(*He looks at* SONNY *with disappointment and challengingly*)

BAI

Yes, I tell them every day, they can at least have a little respect now that Pang is—well—going out. . .

SONNY
(*Insulted*)

All right, all right, old Boela!
What has run over your nerves now? Hey?
(*The* FLOWER SELLER *giggles*)

BOELA

No, nothing runs over my nerves. I'm just saying, you can have a little respect. Let old Pang also listen to the music, man, for the last time. Then he can actually take something with him, when he goes. He really wouldn't want to take that jaw of yours with him when he goes
. . .
(*The* FLOWER SELLER *giggles. Then* PANG *coughs again. It hurts them all. Even* SONNY. MAKIET, *front stage, strong as always, but sad*)

KANNA
That's maybe the last, said Bai.

BAI
That's maybe the last, for Pang. . .

MAKIET
(*Firmly*)

It was the last, for Pang. . .

BAI

Yes.

(Then the "Moses" song is heard)

MAKIET

(Smiles)

Shame, poor Jakop.
> *(She nods her head, smiling at the memory. A pause)*

He liked that song a whole lot.
> *(The music grows in volume. JAKOP appears, his arms raised,*
> *his eyes transported, his wrists red from the suicide, his*
> *presence large and even holy)*

DIEKIE

(Excited) No, no! Jakop! Jakop!

MAKIET

(Smiles pitifully)

It's all right, Diekie. He's coming to fetch Pang. . .
> *(JAKOP to front stage, beside MAKIET. The light is on him,*
> *an other-worldly presence, as he starts to sing. He sings the*
> *song of the people, all of it sacred.)*

(Everyone listens, and they sing along. Halfway through the song PANG coughs, not for long, after which JAKOP continues to sing with power. Finally he exits as he came on. The song dies away. Everyone silent.)

(Eventually BAI's sharp voice breaks the strange silence.)

BAI

That was always Pang's favorite song. . .
> *(His eyes are wet)*

BOELA

Yes.

(He clears his throat)

Yes.

(Disappears into the shop)

(SONNY shifts his hawker's barrow, so that it stands before him beside the porch. He half-sits, half-leans towards the side that opens up to the alley. He sits very still, silent.)

FLOWER SELLER

Carnations!
Red carnations!
White carnations!
Carnations!

TOEFIE

It's goodbye with old Pang, Skoen.

SKOEN

Yes, Toefie.

TOEFIE

Yes, that's the way we all must go, hey. . .

SKOEN

Ja . . .

TOEFIE

It's the doctor.

(BOELA, who has heard the car, comes walking up)

BOELA

(*To* TOEFIE *and* SKOEN)

Is it the doctor?

(BAI *also puts in an appearance again, curious and disturbed*)

TOEFIE, SKOEN

Yes.

BOELA

Yes.

(*He stands a while in thought,* BAI *too*)

KANNA

(*Softly*)

That's the one thing that shuts us all up, Boela said, that makes us quiet. . .

BOELA

That's the one thing that shuts us all up. . .

(SONNY *looks up as if the words are meant for him*)

BAI

Yes.

FLOWER SELLER

(*Subdued*)

Carnations!
Red carnations!
White carnations!
Carnations!

KANNA

Death, Boela said.

BOELA

Death.
(*Offstage,* KIETIE'S *demented laughter is heard, then:*)

FLOWER SELLER

Carnations!
Red carnations!
White carnations!
Carnations!
(*Again* KIETIE'S *laughter.* SONNY, *who remains motionless like the rest, looks up into the sky. Then his head drops. Hands in pockets. The lights upstairs go out.*

KIETIE *enters. She walks past the* FLOWER SELLER. *She's insane.*)

KIETIE

How much for your flowers?
(*She laughs.* MAKIET, *stage front, looks very excited.* KIETIE *to middle stage, then crazy and anxious, breathing hard*)

Ma . . . tell them . . . not tonight. Listen . . . Ma . . . you must tell them
. . . not tonight . . .

MAKIET
(*Agitated*)

Kietie, my child!

KIETIE

Not tonight, Ma . . . I can't . . .anymore . . . Ma . . .

MAKIET

Be quiet, Kietie. . .

KIETIE

Ma . . .I . . .

MAKIET

But Poena. . . Poena will. . .

KIETIE

. . . I can't I can't, Ma, I . . .
(*Then she sits on the railing of the porch where she begins
to draw patterns with her finger*)

MAKIET

Poena will . . . kill us . . .

DIEKIE

He's a bastard! A big bastard!

SONNY

(*With an almost mocking sound in his voice, but also
like some animal howling in the night*)

Tomatoes! Tomatoes! Potatoes! Fresh potatoes!
(KIETIE *laughs again. Then there is the sound of footsteps,
heavy and many footsteps, and menacing.* MAKIET, DIEKIE
and KIETIE *listen fearfully*)

KIETIE

(*Breathless, to* MAKIET)

It's them!!
(*She turns to* DIEKIE)

(*The noise has grown in volume*) (*She is upright, growing hysterical*)

Diekie! Diekie!! Help me. . .Diekie!
(*Sobs and breathes hard*) (DIEKIE *feels inside the waistband of his
trousers. He does not actually show the knife, but lets his hand rest on*

his hip while he stares out before him over the audience—
    a conspicuous gesture) (KIETIE *watching him*)

No, no, not the knife!! Diekie!!
    (*The footsteps coming to a halt suddenly*) (KIETIE *again*)

No!! Diekie, don't!! Not the knife . . .

DIEKIE
(*Without feeling*)

Go to hell, then! Fuck off!
    (KIETIE *screams hysterically, covers her face with her hands,*
        retreats on to the porch)

DIEKIE

You're mad!

MAKIET
(*Echoes*)

Mad!

SONNY

Mad!

FLOWER SELLER

She's mad!

TOEFIE, SKOEN

Mad!

KANNA

Mad, they said. . .
    (KIETIE *sits sobbing on the porch for a while; then she again starts*
        drawing patterns with her fingers) (*Silence, then*)

MAKIET

But even so, she was my child.

KANNA

(*Catching* MAKIET'S *line*)

. . . Makiet said. . .

MAKIET

Even so a person can't just let your child go out like that . . .

KANNA

Even though I know we must all go out, Makiet said. . .

MAKIET

(*Dreamily*)

. . . to just go out like *that*. . . .
(*Silence*)

KANNA

(*He points toward the back of the hall as if indicating a projector,
instructing it to show images*)

Start, then! Show people on their way to work, early in the mornings;
returning home from work, late at night. . . Show Cape Town, busy,
busy. . . An electric power station!
(*Pause*) Show an old woman's hands.
(MAKIET *shows her hands, lets them fall again,
as the siren of an ambulance wails in the distance.*)

KANNA

Show an ambulance, a police van. . .

MAKIET

(*Staring out*)

They come to look at Kietie, and at Poena, too. Then they took Kietie and Poena away, to the morgue. . .

KANNA

For the pathologists. Show the marble slab.

MAKIET

But I asked the police to give Kietie back again, so that I could lay her body out myself, for the coffin and for the funeral. . .

DIEKIE

No, but Ma didn't lay Kietie out. . .

MAKIET

She was my child, after all. . .

DIEKIE

Ma got a heart-attack, can't Ma remember then?. . .

MAKIET

It was a good funeral. You know, there were so many people there. People loved Kietie.

DIEKIE

They were just curious, and Ma wasn't at the funeral, anyway. . .

KANNA

Ma was sick in bed, said Diekie.

DIEKIE

Ma didn't even recognize me. . .

KANNA

. . . until weeks after, Diekie said. . .

DIEKIE

Then Ma had to give the evidence in court. . .
(DIEKIE *suddenly stands at attention, looking straight ahead.*
He speaks as if in court. His voice trembles)

Your Honor!

MAKIET

(*She is telling it now*)

May God forgive me. . .

KANNA

. . . Makiet said. . .

MAKIET

. . . It wasn't all my fault. . .

KANNA

Paans had died on the farm. . .

MAKIET

So there was nothing for us, no, so then we had to move, what could
we have done on the farm. . .

KANNA

baas [master] also said. . . (*Pause*)
So then, they just put their things on the little cart. . .

MAKIET

So then, we just put our things on the little cart . . . (*the* GUITAR
PLAYERS *strumming their guitars, just a little*)
(*Pensively, resigned*)

Then, they caught Kietie when she was little. . . she was only seven
years old. . .

KANNA

And they caught Kietie again when she was big, Jakop's girlfriend . . .

MAKIET

Yes. . .

KANNA
(*Loud*)

Then. . .

SONNY

Tomatoes! Tomatoes!

KANNA

. . . Kietie got a child from the rape, then. . .

MAKIET

Then, Jakop died. . . and Kietie. . .

KANNA

. . . she wasn't right in her head anymore. . .

FLOWER SELLER

Carnations!

MAKIET

Pang was a very good man; he also had the little shop. . .

KANNA

Makiet married Pang, and he made it possible for me, for Kanna, to study further, as they say. . .

MAKIET

Yes.

KANNA

Then Kanna. . . I . . . went away. . .

MAKIET
(Staring)

Then Kanna. . . went away. . .

KANNA

. . . Never came back again. . .

MAKIET

. . . Never. . . came back. . .

KANNA

Then Pang also died. . .
(Light up above)

MAKIET
(Softly)

Then Pang also died. . . Pang. . .
(For a moment, silence; then, as the light upstairs goes on again:)

70

DIEKIE

Not guilty, your Honor! They. . . They. . .
(KIETIE *laughs madly*)

MAKIET

Then Kietie . . . just . . .well . . . married Poena.
(KIETIE *still laughing. She is playing* **klip-klip** *[a child's game with stones, similar to jacks] on the porch, like a child*)

DIEKIE

Your Honor, not guilty . . .

MAKIET

. . . Then I started to find out about the terrible Poena, that he was forcing Kietie to make money for him, with her body, I mean . . .

DIEKIE

He was a bastard, your Honor, a real bastard . . .

KANNA

(*He, too, speaks with the judge, somewhere down there in the audience.* KANNA *is pleading*)

Extenuating circumstances, your Lordship . . .

DIEKIE

Kietie was my little sister, your Honor. . .

KANNA AND DIEKIE

(*Pleading with and for* DIEKIE)

Your Lordship. . .

MAKIET

First, Poena tried to keep me away from the house. I must say, he was very bad, but he always tried to treat me nice. I must say, he was never rude with me. He tried to treat me with respect, after all. . .

DIEKIE
(*Bitter*)

Ma!

KANNA

Your Lordship, Diekie was born again, he . . .

DIEKIE

I was converted. Halleujah!
(*And immediately, together with the guitairs, and like* JAKOP,
*he sings "Come Let Us Sing," but after just a few lines the
song and music stop abruptly*)

DIEKIE

Your Honor, they caught Kietie.
(*Then to the court*) He was a . . . bastard . . . your Lordship!

MAKIET
(*Terror in her eyes now*)

But then, I found out, but I don't know why, I still didn't try to do anything, I can't understand. But Poena was behind it all. He sent the men, to Kietie. For the money, they . . . paid, yes. And Kietie, she was scared of Poena. (*Pause*) And also, Kietie, she was supporting us then, because, remember, Pang was dead. So I didn't try to say anything.

DIEKIE

Ma!

KANNA

... when she was just seven years old, Diekie said, I saw it myself, with my own eyes. . .

KANNA

... Diekie thought, I'll get even . . . With someone, some of them, it doesn't matter who, but with their kind . . . one of the swine . . .

DIEKIE

One day. . .

MAKIET

So I didn't try to say anything, no. (*Pause*) So they got married, and everything, although we were against it all, but. . . Not in church, but in front of the magistrate. . . But still properly married after all. That's the worst of it, that Poena could be so bad after that. . .

KANNA

Your Lordship. . .

DIEKIE

... then they caught our little sister another time, your Worship. . .

KANNA

... Jakop himself saw it happen, again. . .

DIEKIE

Jakop, he loved Kietie. . .

KANNA

He was a preacher. . .

DIEKIE

He was a man of God, your Honor. . .

KANNA

Your Lordship. . .
And Poena was bad. . .

DIEKIE

He was a swine, rubbish, I say. . .

KANNA

Jakop. . .

VOICE

(*Soft, but fills the hall*)

Silence!

DIEKIE

(*Dazed*)

But, your Honor . . . how can it have nothing to do with the matter,
they then caught Kietie. . .
    (*Mocking laughter from the gallery. The* FLOWER SELLER, SONNY *and*
        KIETIE, *all laughing.* DIEKIE *perplexed*)

VOICE

Silence in court!

DIEKIE

But your Honor!

VOICE

Silence!

        (*All is still, then*)

MAKIET

Poena, he wanted to get a lot of money quickly, easily, because he drank, and that costs money, your Worship . . . Also he smoked marijuana, so Poena he didn't work.

(A pause, then earnestly)

The wine and the marijuana do that, your Lordship. . .

(Laughter)

KANNA

Then they hurt Jakop, he tried to fight them off, from raping Kietie . . . Please . . .

DIEKIE

But Jakop, he didn't believe in violence, your Honor must understand . . .

KANNA

He used to say it's no use unless they change themselves!

DIEKIE

Then Kietie came home, crying and crippled. . .

KANNA

And crazy. . . Your Lordship, it's true. . . Diekie is telling . . . truth . . .

DIEKIE

It's true, of course it's true. . .

KANNA

Then Kietie got the child. . .

DIEKIE

From the rape, do you understand!?. . .

KANNA

And Jakop died. . .

DIEKIE

Jakop. . . he committed suicide. . . your Honor, because he was a good man. . . That's why he committed suicide! Because he couldn't *stand* it!
(*Pause*)

MAKIET

Poena then got *really* bad, really terrible, your Lordship, he didn't even *make* with Kietie herself anymore!
(*Repeats so that the court will understand*)

Your Worship knows, *make* with Kietie?! I knew, after all, because their bedroom was right next to the kitchen there. . .
(*Laughter*)

(*Then* MAKIET *thoughtfully*)

Poena, I suppose, made with the other women, somewhere else . . . Somewhere else, yes . . . It wasn't so in the beginning, but later. . . (KIETIE *looks up with huge, sorrowful eyes*) From Kietie, later, he just wanted the money because Kietie she was a pretty girl, your Worship . . . So he forced Kietie to make with the other men, for the money . . . Oh my God . . .

DIEKIE

(*Fearfully*)

Your Worship! So he would just leave Kietie like that, then all the others came, they all came. Sometimes Kietie started to cry, when in the morning, she was there, alone. . .
(*Laughter*)

MAKIET

(*Earnestly*)

Your Lordship, and I didn't try to say anything, Poena he would have killed us, and Kietie. . . No, I didn't say anything, and in the evening they came again! I can show you the bed, your Worship!

(*Loud laughter*)

KANNA

(*Instructing projection again*)

Picture! An old woman with fearful eyes!

DIEKIE

But Ma's giving proper evidence!

COURT

Silence!

DIEKIE

(*Aggressively, interrupting*)

Listen, Pang let Kanna study further so there wasn't any more money, so Kietie had to. . .

MAKIET

(*Fearfully*)

Poena he would have killed us.

COURT

Oh, I think Poena took the money. . .

DIEKIE

He did! . . . Your Honor!

MAKIET

But not all! Because every time Poena came to get the money, he left some for us. . .

DIEKIE

(Begins to see his hopelessness)

But Ma. . . Your Honor. . .

MAKIET

So he wasn't really so bad!

DIEKIE

Ma! He was a bastard, bastard, bastard!

MAKIET

So Diekie, also, always got something . . . from me . . .

DIEKIE

(Helplessly)

Ma! Ma! Sir, you mustn't believe her, sir. Your Honor, Poena's type, they caught my little sister when she was seven years old, so big only, sir *(he shows)*, just so big. Think of that, sir, and Jakop and . . . Ma . . . Sir! *(Plaintively)*

COURT

And . . . you say you were . . . converted?

DIEKIE

(Dazed) Yes! . . . Yes! . . . Sir

VOICE

And you also got some, of the money Poena made, every time. . .

DIEKIE

But I didn't know . . . I didn't know . . .

COURT

That will be all.
    (*Sounds of astonishment, like someone suffocating*)

MAKIET

. . . What, after all, did Diekie manage with the hawking?

KANNA

(*Speaks to the defense*)

Yes, what, after all, did he earn selling the few vegetables, your Lordship?

MAKIET

So I always used to give him a little something . . .

KANNA

So, I ask you to find . . .

MAKIET

. . . of Poena's money . . . He *is* my child . . .

KANNA

. . . extenuating circumstances . . .

MAKIET

Yes.

VOICE OF THE COURT

Extenuating circumstances? When he had premeditated murder since he was, in your own words, so big?

79

DIEKIE

But they caught Kietie! . . .

VOICE OF THE COURT

That will be all.

MAKIET

Poena never told us when he was going to come for the money, but it was always in the evening . . . in the evening, so he could see if Kietie was working . . .
(Commotion in court)

COURT

Silence! Silence!

MAKIET

Kietie was completely scared of him. . .

KANNA

Picture! A pretty girl, ravaged a hundred times . . . more . . . pale face, neglected, pretty still. . . Her fear of death. (*Sounds like drums*)

MAKIET
(She pleads)

Poena!!

KIETIE
(As if reliving it all, but aside, demented)
Poena! I can't. . . any more. . . I . . . Poena! Please, Poena! . . .

POENA
(A voice from the grave)
But the money's getting less and less, dammit, just look here! You're

getting too bloody lazy . . . Just look here . . . So why did you go an'
get pregnant again?! . . .

KIETIE
(She pleads)

But Poena!!

KANNA

Picture! A man creeping down the rickety stairs, to marijuana in the
night, away from the pleading call of his name behind a shut door. .
.

MAKIET, KIETIE

Poena!

MAKIET

Sir, Kietie was really already dead, because she was a farm girl. We
always believed the Bible, so maybe it doesn't matter, she was already
dead . . .

KANNA

Picture! Makiet and Kietie. The bed, a bottle, the Bible, the district.
Picture! Poena in the night. Picture! Kietie. Picture! The men that
Poena sends, the faces of the men that come, in half, in quarter profile.
Picture! The sweaty bodies of the men that come. Again the men that
come. The stairs. Picture! The door to the room.

MAKIET
(Her voice shaking)

Kietie became pregnant again, sir. Believe me, it was Poena's own
child! . . . Then she wanted to do some other work again. But Poena
said no, there's no money in that, there's no profit in that. No, he
didn't want to understand at all. The **dagga** had him, I say . . .

DIEKIE

The swine!

COURT

The swine?

DIEKIE
(*Quickly*)

The bastard!

COURT

Ah, you call him a swine!

DIEKIE

(*Again*)
The swine, yes!

KANNA

No!

DIEKIE

Why do they listen to the old woman, then. . .

KANNA

Diekie, it's Ma . . .

VOICE

Because it's a nice story. And people . . . like a nice story . . .
(*Laughter*)

KANNA
(*Shakes his head*)

No!

(*A pause, then*)

MAKIET

(*Clearly*)

No, I don't want to talk Kietie's guilt away, it can't be talked away, I suppose, but then she really couldn't any more, do you hear me, sir? Because she was going to have a baby again. . .

(*Laughter*)

. . . So I stopped them that night, and I explained to them. . .
(*Laughter*)
. . . and guess what, they all left, they had respect for me, I can't complain. . .

(*Laughter*)

. . . Then . . .

(*Sounds like drums*) (MAKIET, *staring, terrified*)

Then. . . Poena came, the same night. . .

(*For a moment, silence. Then the coughing from upstairs again*)

That same night Poena came and, well, he didn't actually say anything. No, he went actually to be with Kietie, I thought. . .

(*Commotion*)

I was so happy, because that didn't happen for a long time, as I explained. And Kietie, she said nothing, she was also glad, I suppose, that Poena came to her . . . But that was just the mistake she made . . .

DIEKIE

(*Pleads*)

Sir! (*Helplessly*) Aren't you listening? . . .

MAKIET

Well, when he was finished with her, he got up from Kietie. But he was crazy from the marijuana, I say! Oh, he said to Kietie, in his big voice. I thought you were too tired, that you couldn't work. Then Kietie got as pale as the sheet on the bed . . .

DIEKIE

That's why I . . . I . . . the bastard! . . .

COURT

Killed Poena? Smashed his head in?

DIEKIE

Your Worship!

COURT

Dick Davids!

DIEKIE

Your Worship!

(Silence)

COURT

Do you have anything to say before . . .

MAKIET

Strange, that wasn't a time when I had trouble with my heart, but only the time when I laid out Kietie's body . . . for the coffin . . . But, guess, the night . . .

DIEKIE

(Softly, dumbfounded)

Your Lordship, Ma didn't lay Kietie's body out, because Ma was sick in bed . . . It's the first time now, that she's up, here in court. . .

COURT

Do you have anything to say . . .

KANNA

Picture! An old woman in a corner of the room, the fear of death in her eyes. Show Kietie, white as the sheet on the bed. Show the shielding hands, the pleading faces, that's right! (He indicates) And mouths screaming without sound. . .
(The guitars begin to play softly)

DIEKIE

No, your lordship. . .
(Lets his head drop)

MAKIET

I wondered that night what Poena was going to do to me, and guess, in the end he didn't do anything at all, he didn't even so much as look at me. Completely like he never even saw me at all.
(Softly, then slowly, a vision of the story's terror)

He just took it down, from its hook behind the kitchen door, the police later took it away, for evidence . . .

COURT

The police took it away, after Diekie. . .

MAKIET
(Quickly)

Yes, sir. . .

COURT

. . . grabbed it out of Poena's hands, Poena who was acting crazy, and hit him with it, smashed his head *in*. . .

MAKIET

. . . Diekie grabbed it from Poena, yes. . . but after Poena. . . had *hit* Kietie with it. (*Then screaming*) He killed her, that evil Poena! . . He killed Kietie, my child, that night!. . .

COURT

You saw it?

MAKIET

(*Transfixed*)

Yes!. . . the police they took it away. . . .

COURT

Thank you.

MAKIET

(*Near hysterical*)

Oh, Lord God, help me, Kietie was screaming the whole night through. The whole night through, from the pain. . . It was only in the morning that she went out . . . I mean the life in her. . .

COURT

Dead?

MAKIET

Yes, out. . .

COURT

But Poena. . . died quickly?. . .

MAKIET

Yes. Diekie. . .

COURT

. . . grabbed it from that evil Poena, and hit him hard with it, yes?

MAKIET

Yes. . . At first I didn't even know that Diekie was there in the house. I first saw him. . .

COURT

Thank you.

(*To Diekie*)

Dick Davids, do you have anything to say. . .

MAKIET

. . . I don't know when Diekie went out there. . . Diekie my child, he was then my only child, Diekie. . . (*She's hysterical*) Poena, he was dead . . . yes . . . Kietie, she was screaming the whole night through. Then Kietie went out, Kietie was dead, and when I looked, I saw the place . . . there . . . where Kietie was pregnant . . . sir. . . Poena he . . . chopped her where the child was sir! O, Lord God, help me!

KANNA

Is this it?. . .

(*He raises his hand*)

MAKIET

(*Gasps*)

the little axe. . .

(KANNA *drops his hand*)

COURT

Dick Davids. You will hang by the neck. . .
(DIEKIE *stares, confounded. His lips move, he finds no words.*)
(*Silence*)

KANNA
(*In a dream*)

. . . Hang by the neck . . . they took him away, to Pretoria. Diekie. They sent him by train, to death row. Makiet went to the station to. . . see him off. . .
(DIEKIE *remains staring;* MAKIET, *too, her face twisted*) (*Silence*)

MAKIET
(*A tower of strength, now—a phenomenal kind of power is here. Yet, at the same time, an image of utter helplessness*) (*Raises her hand slowly as the train whistles and starts moving. She waves*)

Goodbye. . . Diekie . . . Goodbye. . .
(*The train moves*) (MAKIET *majestically even now*)

Diekie. . .
(*Now* DIEKIE *also raises his hand. It is limp with dejection, but he waves. After all, it is* MAKIET, *there, in the wheelchair, on the station platform*) (MAKIET *waves a handkerchief, she cries, but softly. She gazes after the train as it travels. Then* DIEKIE *is gone.*)

FLOWER SELLER
(*Softly*)

Carnations!
Red carnations!
White carnations!
Carnations!
(*Light appears in the windows above.* BOELA *comes hurrying up the street, in fright.* BAI *appears from inside the shop. They look at each other, questioningly. The* GUITAR PLAYERS *sit up.* SONNY *dejected,* KANNA, *too.* MAKIET *still waving*)

(*Then* TOEFIE *and* SKOEN *on. They start dismantling the scene, slowly, indeed respectfully, section by section.*)

MAKIET

(*Who peers out before her with the half-blind eyes*)

What are they doing, Kanna?

KANNA

(*Helplessly, hastily, without lifting his head*)

Nothing, Ma. . .

(*Pause*)

MAKIET

Don't tell me false things, Kanna!

KANNA

(*Resigned*)

Yes, Ma. . .

FLOWER SELLER

Carnations!
Red carnations!
White carnations!
Carnations!

> *Then, as the guitars sound up, the stage lights fade. In the half-light, TOEFIE and SKOEN carry the set pieces away, off stage. BOELA and BAI follow them out. The FLOWER SELLER and SONNY, too, she with her batch of flowers on the head, he with his barrow of vegetables— a small funeral procession. Then KANNA and MAKIET. KIETIE remains on stage, though—on the porch, above. She starts laughing, a mad, mad laughter.*

(*Echoes.*)

(*But at last all grows dark as the music grows in volume.*)

7. Kanna Is Coming Home

(The music—"Come Let Us Sing"—continues for some time. The dream grows deeper. At last the music fades. As the lights come up, stage empty. Silence. For a moment the audience experiences this silence, a telling wordlessness. Then YSIE and JIENA on, quietly. Their footsteps are hollow and echoing. They place two wooden trestles, for an imaginary coffin to rest on, slightly at an angle mid-stage. The light contracts, and the trestles are imprinted in the audience's consciousness. In the background, a death march.

Then MAKIET'S voice is heard out of the past. Powerfully, peacefully, finished with suffering, majestically. A great mother. The light shines faintly.)

MAKIET
(Questioningly)

Kanna?

   (There is no reply) *(Again, searching for him)*

Kanna?

    (Still no reply)

   (Then commanding)

Kanna!

 (And KANNA answers from the void. His voice soft, far away, full of fear)

KANNA

Yes, Ma. . .

MAKIET

Do you still remember this wind, Kanna?

   (Silence. The wind comes up)

90

And Diekie, Kanna? Our Diekie?
> (*Small footsteps. A gasp. A child cries. Or is it the wind?*)

VOICE
(*From the past*)

It's Kietie, Mamma! It's Kietie! They. . .

ROESLYN
(*From the deep*)

Diekie, didn't I tell you to shut your mouth, hey?

DIEKIE
(*Softly*)

The bastards! Bastards! Swine! (*He cries*)

MAKIET

Diekie, my child . . .
> (*Then the wheels of the donkey cart rolling once more over the cobble-stones*)

DIEKIE
(*Laughing*)

We're all riding together, now!

MAKIET

It's been a long time, the years, Kanna. . .

KANNA
(*Closer*)

Yes, Ma. . .

BOELA

(A voice of years gone by)

You talk too much, Sonny. That's your problem, that you talk too much. Too much, I say, yes.

SONNY

Okay, ol' Boela, okay . . . And I didn't come back, not until now, for your funeral . . .

(YSIE and JIENA on, over KANNA's voice. They are dressed darkly. Each carrying a lighted candle. They go up to the trestle heads, place the candles and stand there—as if the old woman is lying in state)

KANNA

Jiena and them, they let me know again. I came immediately.
(People from the district, children too, enter. Quietly, they go up, one by one, to the trestle heads, to see the old woman in death, some of the children standing on their toes. Then all are standing grouped behind YSIE and JIENA. The light is very faint now. Only the candles burn)

KANNA

(His other I)

But you didn't go for Kietie, and you didn't go for Diekie, and you didn't go for Roeslyn, you didn't even go for Pang . . .
(Then powerful organ music: "Abide with Me." The hall is filled with it. It is the funeral service. YSIE and JIENA stand erect and sad, but not crying. The candles burn. The group behind starts humming as a choir: "Abide with me.")

(When the hymn fades, the little group remains standing reverently, and the voices continue)

KANNA

They took me in. From the orphanage. I grew up. . .
(The tempo of the dialogue is measured to precision)

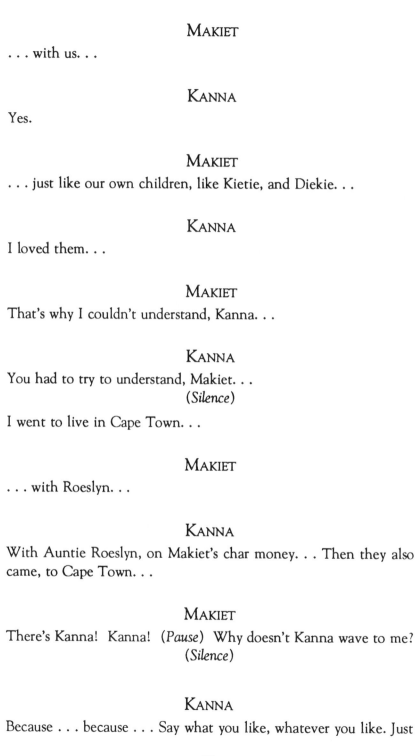

MAKIET

. . . with us. . .

KANNA

Yes.

MAKIET

. . . just like our own children, like Kietie, and Diekie. . .

KANNA

I loved them. . .

MAKIET

That's why I couldn't understand, Kanna. . .

KANNA

You had to try to understand, Makiet. . .
(*Silence*)
I went to live in Cape Town. . .

MAKIET

. . . with Roeslyn. . .

KANNA

With Auntie Roeslyn, on Makiet's char money. . . Then they also came, to Cape Town. . .

MAKIET

There's Kanna! Kanna! (*Pause*) Why doesn't Kanna wave to me?
(*Silence*)

KANNA

Because . . . because . . . Say what you like, whatever you like. Just don't say that Kanna didn't wave because Kanna didn't love you. Don't—

(*The choir again, softly for a moment*) (*Then the voices*)

KANNA

Ysie and Jiena and them let me know, again. They never forgot . . . Kanna . . .

(*The candles fade. Everyone exits. The trestles are removed. Complete darkness*)

VOICE (YSIE)

Hello! Hello! Issit Kanna Davids? Hello! Issit Kanna Davids? Hello!

KANNA

Hello! Hello!

VOICE

Hello! Kanna, it's Ysie here, from Roeslyn. . . Ysie. Do you hear me, Kanna?

KANNA

Hello! Hello!

JIENA

Hello!

KANNA

Hello!

YSIE

It's about Makiet, Kanna, she's had a stroke, she's dead. . .

JIENA

Hello!

KANNA

(*Aside*)

Dead. Makiet. Makiet is. . . dead.
(*Silence*)

But you didn't go for Kietie, and you didn't go for. . .
(*Immediately*)

But Makiet. . .
But the old woman was really old. . . she was really. . .
(*Again, immediately, angrily*)

The old woman? But it's Makiet! Don't you see?. . .
(*At the telephone*)

Hello! Hello! Yes! I'm coming. Yes, yes, wait for me, tell them to
wait for me, I'm coming!
(*A long and breathless silence. Then the lights come up and* MAKIET,
*blind and silent and wonderful, pushes herself on stage, smiling, almost
triumphant. Staring out over the audience, she speaks. Victoriously.*)

MAKIET

(*Slow monotone*)

Get the house very clean. Kanna he is coming home . . . (*Silence*) Ysie,
Jiena.
(*She doesn't call, simply says their names*)

Will you get the house very clean. (*Pause*) Kanna he is coming home.
(*Smiles*) (*Death march*)

(*For a long time just the large presence of* MAKIET. *Then:*)
(*Smiling*)

Roeslyn was wrong, in the end. Kanna did say that he was coming
home, so he *is* coming home, just like he said.
(*Death march and silence*)

Toefie. Skoen. You will go and fetch Kanna from the airport. He won't know the way. He doesn't know the township. He still only knows District Six.

(*Death march*)

KANNA

They did. Toefie and Skoen. They came to fetch me, from the airport. (*The light now falls sharply on rows of municipal houses suggested in the background. There is the sound of a jet plane's landing. MAKIET, stage front, smiles in her chair as she moves off*)

(*Announcements at the airport*)

When I stepped out onto the tarmac (*Kanna now appears on stage*) I found them there, amongst the other people.
(TOEFIE *and* SKOEN *on, reluctant and shy. They are dressed conspicuously in their best, and are ill-at-ease*)

TOEFIE

(*Hesitates*)

Kanna?. . .
Kanna?. . .
(*They wave uncertainly. They look around, aware of how people are staring*) (KANNA *has swung around. He stares, dumbfounded, and as he stares, speaks almost absent-mindedly*)

KANNA

The two hawkers, the two hawker children of Roeslyn, sporting neat neckties!

(*He raises his hand slowly, waves also uncertainly*)

(TOEFIE *and* SKOEN *wave again, as if reassured*)

The two hawker children of Roeslyn came to fetch me, from the plane, at the airport, with their horse cart . . . their hawker's cart . . . (*Pause*) God, the people stared. They were in everybody's way. They bumped into people who got annoyed with them and looked at them with amusement. (*Pause*) I didn't know at first what to do with myself, with them . . . I walked into the Arrivals Hall, I tried to . . . smile . . .

(*He raises his hand again and waves slowly*)

I wasn't . . . expecting Toefie and Skoen there. God knows why not. I must have . . . I might have known . . . that they would be there. . .

TOEFIE, SKOEN

Hey, Kanna! Kanna!

TOEFIE

(*Who thinks* KANNA *is looking around because* KANNA *is searching for the other members of the family*)

No, Ysie and Jiena them couldn't come with, because they're looking after the coffin . . .

SKOEN

(*Uneasily*)

They're waiting for you at the house.
(KANNA *buries his face in his hands for a moment*)

TOEFIE

It's just a short way. We're not up there in Cape Town any more, but down here, in the township, in the scheme. . .

KANNA

I would have taken a taxi. I had the address. I knew they didn't live up in District Six any more. . . A taxi. . . (*then loud*) But Toefie and Skoen have come to fetch you! (*Then imitates them*) No, Ysie and Jiena them couldn't come with, because they're looking after the coffin . . . (*He laughs, loud and long. Then waves. Waves! It is as if he has undergone a metamorphosis*)

KANNA

Hey, Toefie!   Hey, Skoen! Hey!
(He runs towards them, dumps his imaginary bags, and grabs their
hands) (TOEFIE and SKOEN surprised, laugh uneasily)

(Aside)

The people stared!
(To TOEFIE and SKOEN, unnecessarily loud)

How are things at home?

TOEFIE
(Uneasily)

No, it's. . .

SKOEN

. . . going all right. . .

TOEFIE

. . . okay. . .

KANNA
(Aside)

God, how the people stared!

TOEFIE

We're really very glad . . .

SKOEN

Ysie and Jiena. . .

(Loud)

I'll just get my things quickly, then we're off. . .
(He laughs loudly—also a bitter, sad, and ironic sound about his voice.
He crosses over to the other side of the stage, and stands in an imagi-
nary line)

I'll just queue here quickly. Then we can go. . .
> (*He moves a step forward*)

Then we can go . . . (*Aside*)
A thought suddenly struck me.
> (*His attention is diverted, someone has tapped his shoulder from behind*
> *to let him know he could move forward. He turns round, understands,*
> *moves forward*)

Excuse me . . .
> (*Then to* TOEFIE *and* SKOEN)

Just wait for me, I'm almost finished, then we'll be off . . .

KANNA

> (*He speaks their colloquial*)

**Dis mos maar 'n klein entjie kos ons bly mos nie meer in die Kaap
daarboekant nie** [It's only just a little way because we don't live up
there in the Cape anymore.]
> (TOEFIE *and* SKOEN *taken aback by* KANNA'S *switch of language*)

> (*Aside quietly*)

The thought hit me. Do you know what it means for them to come
and fetch you . . . from the airport?
> (*Forward another step, and then to* TOEFIE *and* SKOEN:)

Just hang on, there's just one more person in front of me, then we'll
go. (*Loud*) I'm glad things are still okay at home, also with Jiena and
Ysie. . .

TOEFIE

They're just looking after the coffin. . .   251074

SKOEN

But they're waiting for Kanna. . .

KANNA

. . . at home. Yes, dear God! It means that they're losing a day's work,

the few pence from a day's earnings from hawking. . .
> (*Again pushed from behind,* KANNA *now collects his baggage from the counter.* TOEFIE *and* SKOEN *at a distance, too shy to help him*)

A whole day's earnings. . .
> (*Then to* TOEFIE)

Toefie, how many children have you got now. . .?
> (TOEFIE, *somewhat embarrassed*)

I say, how many children have you got?. . .

TOEFIE

Seven, Kanna . . .

KANNA

Oh. And Skoen?

SKOEN
> (*Uneasily*)

I've got five, Kanna. . .

KANNA
> (*Quietly*)

Do you know what it means for them to come and get you!
> (*He takes the bags down*)

Thank you! Thank you!
> (*A pause. Then, aside*)

Why don't you let the two boys give you a hand, said someone. Those two there. . . The boys, I screamed! (*Agitated*) The boys? But they're my family! (*Then loudly*) Don't you know it's Toefie and Skoen, can't you see? Ysie and Jiena would've also come, but they're looking after the coffin, don't you know? Can't you see, it's Auntie Roeslyn's children who's come to get me?!
> (*He laughs and cries. Then he looks around as if someone has spoken to him*)

A taxi? No! Thanks! We're going in Toefie and Skoen's cart. (*Pause*)
What? Wash the windshield for me?! (*Laughs*) I said *cart*, not car!
(*To* TOEFIE *and* SKOEN) Does your cart then have windshields?
(*They all laugh*)

TOEFIE, SKOEN

Windshields.

KANNA

Come!

SKOEN

Here's the cart; Kanna can just climb in.
(*He puts the luggage on the cart in the back. Then he comes to the front,
climbs up the side, next to* TOEFIE *who has already climbed in. Gets in, at
the back, helped on by* TOEFIE. *The three are sitting now,* TOEFIE *and*
SKOEN *in front,* KANNA *behind them, on a box or behind a railing on stage,
suggesting the cart.* SKOEN *has the reins. They move off.*)
(*The horses trot*)

TOEFIE

It was really a long time . . .

KANNA

Yes. . .
(*Silence*)

TOEFIE

They broke down all our houses in District Six . . .

SKOEN

'Cause it became a white group area. They moved all the people
out . . .

(*Silence*)

KANNA

I heard so. . .

TOEFIE

Yes. Kanna won't recognize the place no more.

KANNA

It was a long time, yes. . .

SKOEN

Yes.

KANNA

So they moved all the people out?

TOEFIE

Yes.

KANNA

Oh. . .

SKOEN

Jiena, she works in one of the factories now. Ysie, she makes tea in the offices. They travel in and out on the train from the township, every day. It's far . . .

KANNA

Oh. . .

(*Silence*)

TOEFIE

But they didn't go to work today.

KANNA

Oh. . .

TOEFIE

Yes.

KANNA
(Aside)

'Cause they are looking after the coffin. . .

SKOEN
(Looks at Toefie)

Yes.

(Silence)

KANNA
(Aside, cynically)

'Cause they're looking after the coffin!
(Laughs bitterly. Aside:)

No, because they're waiting for Kanna. Kanna Davids. Because they're waiting to see Kanna again, after all these years . . . (He shakes his head) Because they can't wait any more, to see Kanna, after all this time . . . God!. . .

SKOEN

Yes, we thought we'd just come and fetch Kanna, 'cause Kanna wouldn't maybe find the place. . .

TOEFIE

'Cause the houses, they look all the same. . .

SKOEN

(*Explains*)

'Cause the houses, they look all the same . . .
(*They laugh together*)

(*Silence*)

SKOEN

Nice roads they made, hey, Kanna?
(*He points*)

KANNA

Oh. (*He realizes it's the wrong word, then:*)
Yes. Yes.

(*Silence*)

TOEFIE

That's the new power station, there. It's Athlone! (*Looks and points*)
(KANNA, *in thought, doesn't answer*)

TOEFIE

(*Louder*)

It's the new power station there, Kanna!

KANNA

Oh yes, the cooling towers . . .

SKOEN

Hey?

TOEFIE

Big, hey Kanna!

KANNA

Yes.

(*Silence*) (*As they ride past the towers, they look up*)
(*Not knowing really what to say*)

The barbed wire around there, what's it for?

TOEFIE

Oh, the barbed wire?

SKOEN

It's to keep the people out . . . (*Pause*)
'Cause it's very dangerous inside there!

KANNA

Oh . . .

(*Laughs, suddenly bitter*)

Do you know what I do for a living? What sort of work? Did I tell you?

TOEFIE

No, Kanna.

SKOEN

No, Kanna didn't tell. . .

KANNA

Oh. . .

TOEFIE, SKOEN

No.

(Silence)

KANNA

I'm an engineer!

(He laughs)

TOEFIE, SKOEN

Oh.

(Silence)

KANNA

Yes! I work for a big firm. *(He laughs)*

TOEFIE, SKOEN

Oh. . .

KANNA

Yes!

TOEFIE

I didn't know. . .

SKOEN

We didn't know. . .

KANNA

Yes. I help to put up big businesses . . . Developments . . .

TOEFIE, SKOEN

The what?
Oh. . .

KANNA

Yes! (*He laughs*)
Yes!

SKOEN

It is really a good work, Kanna?
(KANNA *doesn't answer*)

TOEFIE

We're near now . . .

KANNA

Oh. . .
(*He sits expectantly*) (*The horses trot*) (*Then light falls sharply on the little houses*)

KANNA

Kanna can now see for himself, it's better that we came to fetch Kanna, 'cause the houses they all look the same, like. . .

KANNA

But I have the number . . .

SKOEN

(*As if he didn't hear*)

. . . Just a few more streets!
(KANNA *stares around, doesn't reply*)

TOEFIE

Ysie and Jiena and them are maybe wondering already. . .

SKOEN

They're looking after the coffin. . .

TOEFIE

Yes, we thought we better go and fetch Kanna . . .

SKOEN

It's really a nice day. . .

TOEFIE

(*Sits straight up, excited*)

The bloody kids in the street!

SKOEN

Hey, get the hell out in front of the horses, little bloody stupids!
(*Suddenly realize what they're saying in front of* KANNA, *they clear their throats.* KANNA *doesn't speak.*)

TOEFIE

Makiet had the stroke . . . (*turns to* SKOEN)
When was it?. . .

SKOEN

Almost just like Mama. . .

TOEFIE

Oh, Kanna works for a power station?. . .

SKOEN

Yes. . . It's a good thing that it's such a nice day, so we could go get Kanna by the airport. . .

TOEFIE

Yes. . .

(The light analyzing the township. KANNA stares)

It's a good thing Kanna's wearing a hat, for the sun . . .
(But KANNA doesn't wear a hat!)

Too bad; poor Makiet . . .

TOEFIE

But we looked after Makiet very well . . .

SKOEN

It's a nice coffin. . .

TOEFIE

Makiet was in the burial fund, after all. . . The policy was actually paid up . . .

(Pause)

TOEFIE

Makiet was unconscious the whole time. . .

SKOEN

Yes. She didn't even ask for Kanna. . .

TOEFIE

(Looks hard at SKOEN, then loud to cover up SKOEN's indiplomacy)

It's number one hundred and thirty, now. Just five more numbers. . .
(KANNA anxious) (Silence)

(Death march up, softly)

(YSIE and JIENA enter, slowly, from opposite directions. As if they're gazing out of a window, finally)

109

YSIE

(*Her voice trembling and breathless*)

It's Kanna! . . .

JIENA

(*Almost whispering, staring*)

It's Kanna!
(KANNA *and* TOEFIE *and* SKOEN *climb down from the cart.* TOEFIE *is busy with the horses for a while.* KANNA, *staring, stands and waits uncertainly. Then they approach* YSIE *and* JIENA—*first* SKOEN, *then* KANNA, *then* TOEFIE. KANNA *stops.*)

SKOEN

(*uncomfortably to* YSIE *and* JIENA)

It's Kanna. . . we've just come from the plane. . .
(KANNA *smiles in the direction of* YSIE *and* JIENA)

YSIE, JIENA

(*Completely out of their depth*)

Yes. . . it's . . . Kanna. . .
(*They look. And look, remaining at a distance*) (*A few women from the area enter. But they remain aside, curious but uncomfortable*)

(*In the direction of the women*)

It's Kanna, of Makiet.
(*Silence*)

VOICE

(MAKIET's, *clear and dominant*)

Ysie! Jiena! Is the house quite clean?
Toefie! Skoen! Did you fetch Kanna?
(*Silence.* MAKIET's *presence over all*)

YSIE

(*Uneasily*)

It's really nice that Kanna could come . . . home.
We're really glad that Kanna is . . . here again at home . . .
(*Silence*)

JIENA

How long is Kanna going to stay, Kanna? . . .
(*Silence, then:*)

KANNA

I . . . I'm getting the plane back home, again tomorrow . . . I must .
. . return again, tomorrow . . .
(YSIE *and the others look at each other, their world more broken even than before*)

JIENA

Oh . . . So Kanna is going back again tomorrow. . .
(*At last, to break the awful silence:*)

SKOEN

Does Kanna maybe want to see the coffin?
(KANNA *looks at him helplessly*)

YSIE

Toefie, take the lid off, so Kanna can see Makiet. . .
(TOEFIE *to the middle. He starts unscrewing the cover section of the coffin. Lifts it off, puts it down on the bottom section. Then stands to one side, quietly, reverently, All stare.* KANNA *stands nonplussed*)

JIENA

Kanna can just go look. . . there's Makiet. . .
(KANNA *approaches the coffin, in a state of trance.*

Then he sees the old woman, kneels, bends down, his head over her dead face, and softly cries.

Then MAKIET *on for the last time. She pushes herself in, very slowly, until right beside* KANNA. *Looks at him, her face now right next to his. He looks into her blind eyes. Tears welling in his own. The audience sees her face clearly, and how she is smiling.*

The others exit, slowly. The story has been told. Or not quite.

KANNA *and* MAKIET *alone. Then she lifts her right hand and lets her fingers run through his hair. The light only on this act—of blessing, or what? A shining core of light. . .)*

(Fade out)

THE END

Afterword

South Africa has its share of famous writers of different races. The best known are Alan Paton, Nadine Gordimer, Athol Fugard, Alex La Guma, Bessie Head, Ezekiel Mphahlele, and J.M. Coetzee. Their prominence is, in part, attributable to the fact that they write in English. On the other end of the spectrum is the group of writers who write in Afrikaans, such as Uys Krige, Van Wyck Louw, Opperman, Visser, and duPlessis. Of course, Andre Brink, who writes both in Afrikaans and English, bridges the gap.

According to Professor T.J. Haarhof, "an interesting development is the emergence of colored [mulatto] poets in Afrikaans such as S.V. Petersen and P.J. Philander in whom the pathos of their people is poignantly expressed. There is also the Jewish poetess, Olga Kirsch, who is concerned with the problems of Israel and uses a graceful Afrikaans."[1] Also worth noting are the black writer A.N. Fula's two novels in Afrikaans dealing with the black predicament, *Met Erbarming O Here* and *Johannie Giet die Beeld*.[2]

Kanna—He Is Coming Home was originally written in Afrikaans (a language derived from seventeenth-century Dutch, the language of the original White settlers from the Dutch East India Company[3]). Adam Small, himself a "non-white"[4] South African, has written several works in Afrikaans, uniquely capturing the character, experiences, frustrations, and dilemmas of the Cape Colored, a group of the underclass, many of whom lived on the outskirts of the city of Cape Town, devoid of decent amenities. Small currently works in English, probably to reach an international audience. The insular nature of the Afrikaans language has led to widespread protest, as seen in the 1976 Soweto riots, when Afrikaans was mandated as the language of instruction in black secondary schools.

Thematically, *Kanna—He is Coming Home* deals with family tragedy (the interplay of poverty, life, and death that has constantly visited the Davids family), the brain drain (since Kanna works abroad as an engineer), the idea of an ungrateful child, and certainly the plight of the colored people, which impinges on the political milieu in which the drama is set. When *Kanna* was originally published, apartheid was clearly in force in South Africa. Segregation was the order in law and in practice, and it affected mobility, housing, marriage, jobs, and social contacts. The philosophy behind apartheid was based on the fact that separate development would naturally foster separate cultural and economic growth of each race. Unfortunately, this development was separate but unequal. One of the most strikingly visible aspects of this political system was the Group Areas Act, which dictated that the races reside separately. Each racial category would live in a separate area. Obviously, those in less affluent areas would become victims of crime, disease, rape, and poverty, as evidenced in *Kanna—He Is Coming Home*. Freedom of movement was restricted since blacks were required to carry an identity pass, a document that engendered a great deal of bitterness and misery, and is featured in the writing of both black and white writers. These pass laws were revoked in 1986.

The physical setting of the drama begins in the Cape farmlands where Paans, Makiet, and the family are farm laborers, similar to sharecroppers. The family then follows Kanna to Cape Town (to District Six, the colored area and part of the city setting) to live with Auntie Roeslyn after the death of Makiet's first husband, Paans. Makiet marries Pang, whose sacrifice and thrift, coupled with Roeslyn's efforts, results in Kanna's education. In actuality, the nature of this play cuts across the South African landscape. Part is set overseas, where Kanna travels for further studies. The two settings are joined both physically and technologically, with use of the telephone and plane. Kanna returns not to District Six, but to the "scheme" and leaves the following day.

Kanna—He Is Coming Home is populated by a variety of characters, almost all of whom belong to the colored race. The only white characters are the **baas** [master] of the farm that Makiet is forced to leave after Paans' death, the saleswoman in the fabric store, and Kietie's employer. The **baas's** presence is almost negative, but the two white women are portrayed as bitchy and contemptuous. They see "these people" as a bunch of ignoble savages. When Kietie is raped (for the second time) the employer's attitude is "what can you expect from people like this?" Instead of simple human sympathy, she derides the entire colored race.

Kanna Davids, obviously the protagonist in the play, is described from the outset as brilliant intellectually. He is a foster child, adopted by Makiet and Pang. The emphasis on the fact that Kanna is a foster child signifies that he is an outsider brought into a poor household and, with sacrifice and industry, highly educated. Yet Kanna turns his back on his adopted family when the time comes for him to reciprocate. Kanna's behavior underscores ungratefulness and insensitivity, which almost borders on callousness. The fact that he does not even take a leave of absence from employment to fully honor the woman who made him a professional engineer shows how much of an ingrate he really is.

Kanna's non-leadership is a very important aspect in his character analysis. The comparison with Moses makes Kanna's lack of leadership qualities more poignant. Andre Brink refers to this as the "Moses motif." The Biblical Moses had very little to go by, did not have enough time to prepare for leadership, but when the order came, he rose, answered the call, overcame many adversities, and got his people out of Egypt. Although he did not live to see the land of milk and honey, Moses' initial sacrifice led to the liberation of the entire Hebrew nation. In contrast, Kanna Davids has all the preparation for true political and economic leadership, but again, like Prufrock, he never acts to liberate his people. Knowing Kanna for what he is, we assume he probably would not have ventured even if the people had asked him to lead. He is ashamed of his people, is embarrassed at the airport when Toefie and Skoen (Aunt Roeslyn's sons) give him a ride on a donkey cart instead of a taxi. He seems to feel that his cousins are uncivilized even though they were willing to lose an entire day's earnings to transport him to the new home in the projects. A more sympathetic character would try to reimburse them or to help in some way, at least by giving money to pay for the funeral expenses. The height of ungratefulness comes when Kanna callously announces he is leaving the following day, and since the principal characters directly connected with him—Makiet, Kietie, Diekie, Roeslyn, Pang—

are dead, it is almost certain that Kanna will not come home again.

Jakop, the street preacher and Kietie's fiancé, is a peace-loving person with deep religious convictions who is compelled to act against his religious beliefs. The second rape of Kietie forces him to abandon his non-violent philosophy to fight against seven of the street gang responsible for Kietie's rape. Since the effect of these events has led him to the ultimate betrayal of his beliefs, he takes his own life. Jakop has been a role model for the people generally, but especially for Diekie. His favorite hymn is "Come Let Us Sing/ O Where is Moses."

Pang and Makiet's industry makes possible Kanna's luxury. They are a dedicated, hard-working, self-denying couple who raise Kanna with the hope that he will ultimately make their lot better. Unfortunately Pang dies early in the play and Kanna does not come to the funeral.

Kietie has been a victim of circumstances, the character who has suffered from early childhood until her violent death. Gang-raped at the age of seven and later on as an adult, she marries the punitive, abusive Poena, who further exploits her. Instead of marital bliss, she experiences further violation as she is forced into prostitution to support Poena's addiction to alcohol and drugs. Poena finally murders her when she is no longer able to continue that lifestyle. Despite her own psychological problems, she is a very dedicated, loving Davids family member who does her best to support those around her.

Poena, Kietie's husband, is the most hateful character in the play. He lives up to the epithets applied to him, being wholly despicable, a product of the gutter from which he is spawned.

Diekie, an impressionable, impulsive young man, cannot restrain himself from reacting to the abuse Kietie suffers at Poena's hands. Since the judge will not allow the defense of extenuating circumstances, Diekie's life is sacrificed, just as Kietie's and Jakop's, and in some sense, Makiet's also. Diekie retains his calm dignity even as death approaches. His life seems ruled by inescapable fate.

Aunt Roeslyn's children—good-natured and hard-working—are genuinely interested in helping others. Ysie, Jiena, Skoen, and Toefie are not envious of others' success. They work hard for the little they have and are willing to share with Kanna and others. In a play like Kanna—He Is Coming Home one cannot dismiss such characters as the flower seller and the street vendor. They all form part of the community and it is through them that we see the everyday struggle of those living under a repressive political system. The dramatic function of these minor characters is more than comic relief: the cry "Carnations, Red Carnations" reflects the pain of a horribly traumatic experience at various stages of the drama—at Pang's imminent death, when the surrounding community prepares for the catastrophe, the interjection of the cry "Red Carnations" leads the mind immediately from the tragedy, although the tragic element is still very much in the air. The foghorn and the southeastern wind have the same effect, an important, forceful, dramatic weapon (as in *Death of a Salesman*).

Kanna—He Is Coming Home is complex in terms of style, because of its interplay between life and death, and the time shift between past and present. It is organized into seven divisions: 1. Oh, Where is Moses; 2. Goodbye, Kanna; 3. It's Kietie; 4. So They Put Their Things on the Little Cart; 5. The Oracle of God; 6. Goodbye, Diekie; 7. Kanna Is Coming Home. The first section, a cry for leadership, acts as a prologue in the same sense that the seventh episode, "Kanna is Coming Home," acts as the epilogue. The characters are introduced via a voice on a microphone, who refers to them as "the simple ones; the most simple ones; the poor that will always be with us." The drama shows how the simple, honest, hard-working characters, unfortunately the poorest, try to make life better for the sophisticated professional engineer who, with everything to give and the resources to change the plight of the simple ones, never does. Between the hopeful "Kanna Is Coming Home" and the final "Goodbye, Kanna" is an ironic and satiric message. Suddenly Kanna's homecoming, for which the simple ones had so elaborately prepared with their limited means, has turned to a final farewell as Kanna announces his return overseas. The play constantly alludes to Biblical figures and events and this indicates in most cases that religion, wherever practiced, is presented as an instrument for consolation.

The entire work, structured under the divisions already referred to, constantly shifts time between present and past. The action is seen through Kanna's consciousness. He mentally recreates events in his life prior to his coming home. Most of these events are not pretty ones, since tragedy overtakes the family: the death of Krools, Makiet's firstborn, Paans' death, the journey to the city via donkey cart, Pang's death, the rapes of Kietie, the violent death of Jakop, Roeslyn's hard life, the exploitative behavior of Poena, and Diekie's trial and hanging. In his mind, Kanna keeps on going back and forth, recreating these tragic events for the reader, giving the play a very forceful dramatic power. The characters speak from the dead to the living, even from the grave.

Other devices effectively used in the play are the music of "Come, Let Us Sing," which gives this piece a very lyric, almost operatic flavor. The full power of this device is realized in a riveting stage presentation.

The version of the Afrikaans language used by Small in the original is unique. He uses "Kaaps," the vernacular Afrikaans of the "Cape Colored," to authentically capture the plight of his people living under the yoke of apartheid, where their separate development ensures underdevelopment, a ghetto-like existence that breeds crime, rape, disease, alcoholism, and further poverty. In some sense, Kanna's emigration is perhaps a reaction against a bad political system. Again, like most South African writing in general, *Kanna—He Is Coming Home* is an indictment against the South African policy of apartheid, especially the Group Areas Act where, as a result of legislation, the colored population in the Cape must relinquish their District Six neighborhood. They must move to the "schemes," commuting many miles daily to and from the city.

Repetition (of words, phrases, music) as a dramatic device is a hallmark of the communication pattern in the play and of very simple people. Small has accurately captured this aspect of their lives.

The play is so well-written and well-structured that what could have become melodramatic sentimentality in the hands of a lesser author in Small's hands has become one of the richest theater pieces in the South African *oeuvre*. The original drama *Kanna Hy Kô Hystoe* was performed by a mixed cast in the 1970s, although the time frame the play refers to is the 1950s. The current translation (but with most of the dialect deleted)was staged in 1985 in Cape Town at the Baxter Theater, and then to critical acclaim in Atlanta at Seven Stages Theater. Critical response to Adam Small's *Kanna—He Is Coming Home* has been very positive. Nancy Kearns' review in *Theater Journal* (Vol. 37, Oct. 1985) speaks highly of the play, and the Atlanta critics were uniformly impressed. One of the best critical investigations of the play is by Andre Brink, "I am smilin': sentiment and satire in

Adam Small" (translated in part by C. Lasker), which gives an in-depth analysis of the dramatic characteristics of the play. According to Brink, "the episode named 'Goodbye Diekie' most certainly has no equal anywhere in Afrikaans."[5]
Carrol Lasker
Kwaku Amoabeng

Endnotes

1. Smuts, J. "Afrikaans—Its Origins and Development." Haarhof, T.J. "Afrikaans Litera-ture." *An Encyclopedia of Southern Africa.* Comp. and ed., Eric Rosenthal, 5th ed., London, New York: Frederick Warne, 1979, 7–9.

2. Transl. and ed., C. Lasker, *The Golden Magnet.* Three Continents Press, Washington, D.C., 1984.

3. Wren, Christopher S. "Blacks Shaped Language of Apartheid, Linguists Say," *The New York Times,* May 16, 1989, C1, 11.

4. The political classification of races in South Africa is in two basic groups: White and non-White (i.e., Blacks, Colored [Mulatto], Asians).

5. *Ons Erfdeel: Algemeen-Nederlands Tweemaandelijks Kultureel Tijdschrift,* Belgium, 19 (1976): 549–61.

Some Titles in the Series

JAMES J. WILHELM
General Editor

1. Lars Ahlin, *Cinnamoncandy.*
   Translated from Swedish by Hanna Kalter Weiss.

2. *Anthology of Belgian Symbolist Poets.*
   Translated from French by Donald F. Friedman.

3. Ariosto, *Five Cantos.*
   Translated from Italian by Leslie Z. Morgan.

4. Enrique Medina, *Las Tumbas.* Translated from Spanish
   by David William Foster.

5. Antonio de Castro Alves, *The Major Abolitionist Poems.*
   Translated from Portuguese by Amy A. Peterson.

6. Li Cunbao, *The Wreath at the Foot of the Mountain.*
   Translated from Chinese by Chen Hanming and
   James O. Belcher.

7. Meïr Goldschmidt, *A Jew.*
   Translated from Danish by Kenneth Ober.

8. Árpád Göncz, *Plays and Other Writings.*
   Translated from Hungarian by Katharina and
   Christopher Wilson.